Tiger Mine

Angela Castle

Published by Rogue Phoenix Press

ISBN: 978-1-936403-83-7

Credits

Cover Artist: Gemini Judson

Editor: Christie L. Kraemer

Printed in the United States of America

Dedication

I fell in love with my characters and it was a hard to let go, once I finished. I hope you enjoy reading it as much as I enjoyed writing it.

Chapter One

Desperation was becoming a prevalent emotion in Mohan's life. With each passing moment, he slipped deeper into the unwanted state.

His food supply was limited, and he grew weaker with each passing week. Soon, he would be forced into the situation of journeying back into the human populace. It was dangerous for a creature in his situation.

As long as he remained in animal form, he had a chance of surviving. Yet, with each necessary shift to his human side, he grew weaker. His body ached with a gnawing hunger. Even in the warm climate of this new land, he was cold.

Mohan had been fortunate to find shelter; an old, abandoned farmhouse. It had several rooms and would have once been a comfortable home. Someone had left it to the ravages of time and was in need of much repair.

He would restore it if he had the resources. For now, it was a roof over his head and kept out the chill of the cold mountain nights. Still, even with a full blaze in the solid stone fireplace, it only partially kept the chill from his bones.

He had nothing with which to trade, nothing to barter, and he had limited English. All he would need to do was open his mouth to speak, and they would know he was not of this land. The clothes on his back he had taken from a pile discarded next to a large bin on a seaside street, near where he had come ashore. By day he had walked over many fertile, abundant fields through strange forests. As darkness fell, he had shifted and used the strength of his animal form. He hunted rabbits to help him continue on. As he moved further away from people and higher into the mountains, the safer he began to feel.

Stumbling across the farmhouse had been an answer to an unspoken prayer. He had collapsed in the old building, staying still until his exhaustion had faded.

His sleep was fitful, filled with nightmare images. The smells and screams in his head plagued him. He would never forget the pain and helplessness of everything he'd been forced to endure.

Why did he fight for survival when he had nothing to live for?

Mohan's natural instincts were more often a curse than a blessing. It was only natural to fight to survive.

The late afternoon sun filtered through the mountain trees. Already the air was beginning to cool.

Counting the days, he knew a few months had passed since he'd come to be here. His clothes were tattered and worn thin. He balanced the heavy load of wood he had collected for the fire. When dusk fell, he would hunt rabbits to feed his hunger then settle for the night.

He was still a distance from his cottage. His feet easily found the track back to his shelter. Deep in thought, he had not heard anyone or anything approach. His hearing was less acute while he was in human form.

He froze at the line of trees surrounding the old house. There was a large dark vehicle parked out front and attached to the back was a covered trailer.

Quietly, he lowered himself into a crouch and set down the wood. His eyes trained on the open door of the house. A figure appeared there.

The baggy, pale blue, short-sleeved top and jeans did not hide the fact the wearer was a generously curved woman. A cascade of light auburn hair fell about her shoulders, gleaming in the last of the fading sunlight.

He noticed the old tarp he'd been sleeping on was carelessly tossed out and now lay by the end of the porch, along with a heap of old ruined and unusable furniture.

Mohan's jaw clenched in displeasure. What was he going to sleep on now? He waited and continued his observations.

There was no one else as far as he could tell. The woman proceeded to unpack the trailer, carrying box after box into his current home.

It was clear he had just lost his shelter. There would be no fire to warm his side tonight. He would be forced to move on.

Rising to his feet, Mohan curled his fingers so tightly around the slim tree by his side his whole hand throbbed. He welcomed the pain as he battled to bring his anger under control.

Forced. He was so tired of being forced to do things he did not want to do. He needed to regain some control, take back the little comfort he had managed to claim as his. Mohan faded unseen into the thick of the trees. He would wait until dark. He would not give up his new home so easily, and one lone woman would not stand in his way.

~ * ~

Julia Cooper's groan echoed around her grandfather's old empty house.

"It's worse than I remembered," she muttered to no one particular, gazing at the decay and dust of the main room. Floorboards creaked under her weight as she moved around inspecting everything. She pinched her nose to hold back the sneezing fit, with the dust tickling her nose.

She glanced down at an old tarp someone had placed in front of the fireplace. The whole area seemed free of dust and the ashes in the fire grate appeared fresh, recent. Someone obviously had been squatting.

The work seemed overwhelming, she had half a mind to turn around and drive back.

Julia swallowed the lump forming in her throat, thinking back over the messy divorce. It was why she was here.

Ending her six-year marriage had left her tired, both emotionally and physically. Every place in the suburb of Kew she visited or needed to go around, left her with raw painful emotions as if salt had been rubbed into the wounds Richard left in her life.

She could no longer stand the look of pity in her friends' eyes. Nor could she stand the continued condemnation from her mother, telling her divorcing Richard was a mistake and she should take him back despite his infidelity.

She needed a place to breathe, a place to let go, a place where she could pull herself together again and contemplate what she wanted to do with the rest of her life.

Only one place came to mind. The one place of comfort in her life had been with her grandfather when she was young. When he passed away, he had left Julia his property with the old farmhouse up in the Snowy Mountain Ranges.

So far, her plan was simple: she would throw everything she had into fixing up the old place then she would decide what to do. After all, it could take months, even years, until she got the place the way she wanted it.

It was going to take more than just a hammer, a few nails, and a lick of paint to get this place up to scratch. The repair list grew with each thing she inspected.

"No, I won't let them win," she reassured herself aloud as she currently had no one else to talk to. "I won't quit."

She cleaned off the kitchen benches with her arsenal of cleaning products and set up her camping stove. Then set out her camp kitchen and cooking equipment.

Any furniture that was beyond usable, she tossed out the front door.

She was grateful for her foresight to buy what she hoped was a comfy double bed. It would fit nicely in her grandfather's old room--once she got it in out of the trailer and assembled. She swept the floor as best she could, set up a gas lamp then unfolded a card table and its accompanying chairs.

Julia worked like a woman possessed to get things cleaned up as much as possible, but she became despondent that much of the work still needing to be done was beyond her skills. She would need a carpenter, a plumber, a general handyman, and an electrician for the wiring and to get the generator she had ordered up and running.

Tired, Julia got the new bed out of its cardboard box and placed all the parts on the bedroom floor. She stomped out to the trailer and battled with the mattress to move it through the short door. With a grin of triumph, she propped it up against a wall out of the way.

She gripped the Allen key in her hand. Surely it couldn't be that hard to assemble. Her stomach groaned loudly in complaint, as the task of making some dinner won over assembling a bed.

Outside it had grown dark, but right now she needed food. Julia lit the lamps and set the fire using fuel logs she'd brought from a gas station. She smiled to herself, watching the flames flicker while holding out her hands to warm them against the chill.

A plan settled into her mind. She would head into town the next morning and ask around for someone she could hire to help her repair her grandfather's old house.

Her stomach called again. She wandered out to her Rover for the last time that night, fetching her icebox full of chilled meat. Her mouth watered as she thought of the juicy steak she had waiting to cook.

She pulled the long icebox from the back seat and set it down as she closed and locked her Rover's doors. Scooping up her icebox, she turned back towards the house. Julia froze. Her eyes became saucer-wide in utter shock. She dropped the icebox stumbling back against the side of the car. Her breath seized in her lungs, and her hands and legs shook. Terror gripped her.

Chapter Two

"Holy crap!" she gasped managing to suck in a lungful of air.

Seated on hind legs at the entranceway to her house was the biggest damn cat she had ever seen outside a zoo--and it was, she knew, a deadly predator. From the lamplight coming from inside her house, she could see it was pure white with bold black stripes, just like the tigers Siegfried and Roy used in their Las Vegas act. What the heck was a white tiger doing in the Snowy Mountain Ranges of Victoria, Australia? Of course, the most worrying thought bouncing around her mind was, *Am I about to become this tiger's dinner?*

The tiger simply stared at her, and she stared back. Julia was frozen. The tiger shifted, moving casually onto all four paws. She thought her heart had stopped. This was it. The tiger was going to attack her. But to her surprise, the big predator ignored her as it smoothly leapt over the broken porch steps and stopped in front of her dropped icebox. The big cat used its left paw to pry off the askew lid and stuck its head into the container.

The cat emerged with her paper wrapped steak between its sharp teeth. Then it turned its back on her and, as casually as a house cat, walked into her new home. The tiger swished its long, white stripy tail up in the air, and from Julia's vantage point behind the cat, it became apparent to her, due to his large package, the cat was male.

Her terror started to ease and was replaced with curiosity. Was it possible this white and black striped tiger was someone's tamed, lost pet? She felt a little indignant the creature had just stolen her steak. Peeling herself away from the rover and avoiding the broken steps, she moved up onto the porch and peered into her house.

The big tiger had sprawled out in front of her fire and was nuzzling at the wrapped meat. He held it down with one paw and ripped off the paper with his large and very sharp-looking teeth.

Trying to stop her legs from trembling, she took a step inside to continue studying the casual looking big cat.

"You know, that was my dinner. If you're that hungry, you could have asked."

He raised his head to stare at her. Julia took a step back in respectable fear. Surely, if it was a wild tiger, it would have attacked her by now.

On a whim, she asked. "I'm getting the sudden feeling you're a tame tiger. Are you?"

It didn't feel so foolish to be talking to the tiger. Maybe the sound of her voice would help soothe it.

The sudden, loud purr confirmed her suspicion. He went back to trying to get at her meat. After shredding the fragile paper, he ate the steak like he hadn't seen one in over a week.

She kept by the open door, just in case he now decided she looked like dessert.

"I've got more food, if you're still hungry."

The beautiful, pale blue eyes of the white tiger stared up at her. His purring became loud again. Slowly, he climbed to his feet and approached.

She knew it was stupid. She clamped her knees together to stop herself from running to the safety of her car and locking herself in until the big cat went away.

She swallowed and pushed back her fear. She couldn't identify the feeling deep within, but something was telling her this big, dangerous, out-of-place tiger would not hurt her.

She held out a trembling hand towards the big cat's muzzle.

"Now, remember, I'm not food but a friend. I really love cats, and you're the most beautiful big cat I've ever seen. Please don't eat me."

In her own ears, her voice sounded a little hysterical. The big cat just pushed against her hand with his face.

Julia was surprised at how soft his fur was. She slid her fingers along the side of his face, up and over his head, carefully stroking him as she would any old house cat.

Without really thinking, she sank down onto her knees. The big cat nuzzled into her, rubbing his big body against hers and almost knocking her over in the process. A giggle bubbled from within as relief poured through her, though the adrenaline rush of fear still made her tremble all over.

"Okay, I get the message: very friendly. You really are a wonder. How the heck did you get so far from home? Are you someone's lost pet? Perhaps I should go and call someone about you."

The cat suddenly pulled away and gave a low growl. Julia fell backwards onto her ass. Her eyes widened with renewed fear as the big cat now towered above her. She got the uncanny feeling he was responding to her words, but how could he know what she was saying?

"Um, okay. I don't have to call anyone if you want to stay lost."

He words seemed to win the tiger's approval. He purred and suddenly licked the side of her face with his rough tongue. Julia relaxed once more as her giggles filled the room.

"Okay, okay, big boy. I think I get it. You want to stay footloose and fancy-free. I won't tell anyone you're here."

He licked the other side of her face. "Stop that. I don't need a bath."

The white tiger turned his big body around and retook his place by the fire. He laid his head on his paws, and Julia climbed to her feet.

"I'll go get the icebox and some more food, okay?"

Her heart was pounding a mile a minute. She must be utterly insane--or hallucinating. A white tiger? Here in Australia? What was she going to do?

As she gathered the spilled and pillaged contents of her icebox, she thought about the whole crazy situation. Was it crazy? Why did she have to do anything other than keep him? Other people had pets, so why couldn't she? What did it matter if he was a big, beautiful white tiger? He was obviously very tame.

She walked back into her cottage and set the icebox on the table. Then she went to close the door.

"I do hope you're housebroken. Let me know if you need to go out and use the bathroom, okay?"

The cat just continued to watch her. She removed the rest of her meats, including the last steak. She unwrapped each package, plonking it all on a big dinner plate before setting it down before the big cat. He didn't just tuck straight into the plate of meat as she had expected him to, but instead glanced up at her as if waiting for something.

"Go ahead. It's not as if I need to put on any more kilos. I'll have some soup and tea."

She could have sworn the cat gave a grunt before rising over the food and swiftly demolishing it. Afterward, he licked the plate clean.

Julia couldn't contain her impish grin. "Good! At least you know how to do dishes."

Purring contentedly, he lay back down and Julia removed the plate.

"I must say; this has been a strange turn of events. I'm Julia Cooper, by the way, and this is my grandfather's old place." Strangely, Julia found it easy to talk to her new tiger.

~ * ~

"I used to come here when I was a girl, but big city life draws you away. Plus, Grandpa and my mum didn't seem to get on very well. A pity, really. It needs a bit of fixing up, but I'm determined to do it."

He listened to the woman talk. It wasn't an unpleasant sound. Her voice was soft and easy on his sensitive hearing. He also approved of the way she had tasted: sweet, womanly. Licking her face had been a smart move.

He watched her putter about, pouring water from a bottle into a kettle before setting the kettle onto a little stove. She flicked a switch, and a flame came to life under it.

Mohan had two courses of action. The first was to scare the poor woman out of the cottage. He knew that action would come with repercussions. She would call for men with guns, and the hunt for his hide would be on.

His second action, although somewhat humiliating, was to pretend to be a tame pet, play upon her womanly sympathies, and ultimately obtain what he needed: food and a place to sleep. He smelled the meat her small, travelling icebox still contained. His mouth salivated in hunger, and his stomach rumbled. He followed through on his second plan.

She had more courage than he thought she would have. She hadn't run screaming, although panic and fear had been there for a moment. He did his best not to appear threatening, and stealing her meat seemed to have endeared him to her. If he played his cards right, he might just get a full belly every night--and a warm, soft place to sleep.

She had a natural beauty about her. To his sensitive nose, she smelled fresh and clean. His gaze ran up over her curves, full without being overly so. He knew if he touched her, she would be soft.

The tightness across her loose shirt indicated a full bosom. Her lovely wide eyes were in proportion to her rounded face and elegant high cheekbones. Her eyes were framed by lovely auburn eyelashes. Her eye colour was a darker shade of blue than his own, reminding him of the deep, wide lakes of his homeland. A blooming colour crept into her cheeks as the air grew more chilled.

The thought ran through his mind that this Julia was just the kind of woman to be held tightly in a man's arms at night, keeping him warm. In his land, she would be a bountiful prize to be won.

Why was she out here alone? Where was her man? The thought made him growl, even before he could stop it. He had trouble understanding the ways of Western men. How could they abandon their bountiful women to pursue stick thin waifs with little intelligence or warmth? In his country, women like that did not survive the cold winter. You had to be strong and smart.

"Um, you okay there, big boy?"

Mohan raised his head and stopped his growling. To ease her sudden, tense fear, he vibrated his throat muscles into another loud purr.

He watched as her shoulders relaxed and she began talking to him about the house and the repairs she wanted to do. It was clear she owned it. She informed him her grandfather had willed it to her after his death.

He was staring at her moving lips as she animatedly talked to him. Her upper lip was a little thin, but it was balanced by a full, soft bottom lip. Mohan tore his gaze from her and stared at the flickering flames of the fire. He should not be thinking about this frail human woman and her very womanly attributes.

Guilt ate at him, and he scolded himself. Feeling guilt over a human? Damn, just how weak had he grown? What if she did report him to some kind of animal hunters? Yet, he was not the kind of man who took without giving something in return.

Every little thing in his life had come with a price. He had earned--and fought--for everything he ever had. But even that had been ripped from him in a matter of moments.

Another plan began to formulate in his head.

"You're going to take a lot to feed," she said absently, ending on a whimsical laugh.

He enjoyed her musical laughter, the way her lips curved at the corners and gave her a more youthful appearance. She lowered herself down into the single blue chair, a steaming mug gripped in her small hands. His sensitive smell told him it was tomato soup. "It's a good thing you've found yourself a wealthy woman."

Mohan's ears pricked up. "My ex-husband would have a blue fit if he knew I was spending all the money I got in the divorce feeding a tiger and fixing up my grandpa's old place."

So, she was no longer mated. *What kind of man lets a prize possession like Julia go? Someone very stupid.* Well, like it or not, he would embed himself into her life. She was someone he needed right now. He needed to make things right to keep the balance.

It didn't matter. As much as he admired her bravery and kindness for letting a tiger into her home, she was off limits. The moment she knew what he was, she would label him a freak like everyone else. Besides, she was *not* his kind.

~ * ~

Julia tossed aside the Allen key and instructions in frustration. Although they were printed in English, it was all Chinese to her.

"Clearly, I'm hopeless at this stuff. Lord knows how I'm going to get everything fixed up," she told the tiger. "Guess sleeping out by the fire isn't a bad idea, hey?" Abandoning the so-called 'easy assembly' bed frame, she climbed to her feet. Damn, her back ached. She stretched it before giving a wide yawn.

She cleared a place in front of the fire. Then she fetched the mattress, and plonked it down before rolling out her sleeping bag.

"I hope you don't snore." The tiger gave her what she was sure was an indignant look. Unfazed, she undressed, shivering with cold, and pulled on her warm pyjamas. She turned down of the gas lamp and wormed her way into the sleeping bag.

The mattress dipped. Julia rolled to encounter her new feline friend lying on the other side, his back presented to her.

"Hey, my bed. Off."

The tiger ignored her. Julia doubted she could move the massive cat. She guessed he must be about three hundred pounds. She sighed. "Fine. But if you hog the blankets, or I wake up to find half my arm missing, you're in big trouble, boy."

Again, there was no response from the tiger. Julia gave another chuckle before closing her eyes. It felt surreal. Who shared their bed with a white tiger? Well, obviously crazy, divorced women did.

Oddly, it was comforting having the big beast next to her. She felt the creature shift closer, his back now pressed against her side, no doubt seeking more warmth. Just like a housecat, she mused.

Not opposed to it, Julia pulled an arm from her sleeping bag and slid her hand through his bountiful fur. So soft and plush. She stroked him, and the low purr of his contentment was clear. With a smile on her lips, Julia fell asleep.

Chapter Three

Moaning, Julia's skin pebbled as something hot, wet and slightly raspy slid over her pert nipple. Good god, it felt so damn good. She arched her back to get closer to the sensation, sending jolting heat waves through her body.

Hot breath fanned across her skin. The wondrous tongue left a trail of moisture in the valley between her breasts. Having found the other neglected nipple, it was now given the same vigilant attention.

The feelings made her belly clench and juices flow between her thighs. She didn't want this dream to end nor the feeling of the man and his tongue that awakened her body. She slid her hand up into his soft plush hair. She loved the feel of it sliding though her fingertips as he continuously lapped.

Cold air made her shiver and awaken further. Julia opened her eyes. Sunshine streaming in from the window haloed the striking white and black colour nestled against her chest. Momentarily confused, she blinked. Then it all came flooding back. This wasn't a man; this was a very large, white and black-striped tiger licking her breasts!

Julia gasped. She uncurled her fingers from his fur and shoved at the tiger.

"Ohhh, bad kitty!" The sleeping bag was snagged around her waist and her pajama top was wide open. The buttons had been torn off--no, not torn off, Julia realized, but bitten off.

The tiger leapt off her and the mattress in one bound. He stalked towards the door, sitting his rear down before glancing over his shoulder, with what she swore was an expectant expression. Julia sat up and yanked the ends of her top together. What the hell had the tiger been doing? Giving her a cat bath? Why the heck would it bite the buttons off her top? She didn't have a scratch on her body, and her chest still heaved with the unexpected sexual stimuli. Good god, she had been turned on by an animal. She felt her face flush crimson.

"Utter madness," she mumbled, shoving the sleeping bag from her legs and rolling over onto all fours before climbing to her feet.

"I am not a cat, if you haven't noticed! I prefer water to a tongue for bathing."

The tiger simply gave her a dry stare. Julia stalked to the door and yanked it open.

He causally walked through it and leapt gracefully off the porch. Then he ran the rest of the way to the line of trees surrounding her house and vanished into the native Australian forest.

An insane fear stole over Julia. She wondered if she would ever see the big cat again. Shivering, she turned back to the house and went inside, slamming the door behind her. Her gaze searched the wooden floor for her buttons. She knew nothing about tigers apart from the odd wildlife documentary on the television. So far all she knew about this tiger was he didn't view her as a meal. And she sure hoped he didn't view her as a potential mate just because he had licked her breasts.

"I am utterly insane," she muttered under her breath as she knelt down and retrieved the pajama buttons.

~ * ~

He growled as he ran, running until his heart thumped painfully against his rib cage. Reaching a clear mountain stream, he slowed and came to a stop by the water. Then he shifted. He shivered in the cool mountain air. His clothes had been washed in the stream and now hung over the branch. Still icy cold, he shrugged into them and welcomed the numbing feeling of the morning dampness. His body heat would help dry them.

What the hell had he been thinking? Actually, he hadn't been thinking--that was the problem. The image of Julia's naked body had stayed in his mind. He hadn't been able to tear his eyes away as she changed clothes, then she had tossed and turned in her sleep.

The sleeping bag had ridden down and the top buttons of her nightshirt had become undone, revealing one side of her lush full breasts. Tempted, he'd nuzzled in, making short work of the rest of her buttons with quick nips of his sharp teeth. The first taste of her skin on his tongue had sent a jolt of pleasure coursing though his body--sweet, salty, womanly. He purred and lapped, wanting to taste more. Her nipples tasted different, tangy, much like the zing you get from biting into the skin of a plum and being rewarded with juicy flesh.

That's exactly what Julia was: a woman he wanted to sink his teeth into, to devour with his body and lap all the juices he could make flow from her.

Her arousal had wafted into his sensitive nose, spurring him on. His body responded, and a hard ache developed. If she hadn't woken, he would have torn off the sleeping bag and shredded her sleep clothing to get to the sweet nectar teasing his senses.

Mohan drew in a deep breath. He couldn't allow that to happen. *Not his people.* The words echoed around in his head. He walked a dangerous line. She mustn't ever become aware of what he was; for most certainly it would mean his end.

He had no desire to see his end yet. He had a plan to put into place. Julia was the first step in a long path ahead.

He knelt down and dunked his head underwater. Coming up for air, he drew in a shuddering breath. He slicked his hair back with his fingers in an attempt to make himself as decent as possible.

Barefooted, he retraced his steps. He had taken a chance with her as a tiger. He hoped she was just as receptive to him as a man.

~ * ~

Names. Julia had been going over them in her head while scrubbing the bathroom. By the look of the showerhead, it would need to be replaced, along with the piping. Well, at least she could get it clean before she had to contemplate that step.

She wanted to call the tiger something other than *big boy*. Naughty kitty came to mind, and for the umpteenth time, she felt the heat rise into her cheeks. Damn it to hell, she couldn't stop thinking about the way it had made her feel.

She scrubbed harder on the same spot, over and over, not really paying attention to what she was doing. A sudden knock at the door made her jump out of her skin.

"Crikey, James and Joseph!" Her heart still pounding in her chest, she climbed to her feet. She hadn't heard any car approaching. Who the heck could be at her door? Pink rubber gloves still encased her hands as she marched through the house and yanked open the front door.

Julia blinked in stunned surprise. She wasn't sure what the right word was, but beautiful was the only one that came to mind as she stared up into a pair of clear, pale blue eyes. She was instantly reminded of her tiger lodger. The man's ink-black hair hung to his shoulders, and he looked liked he'd been swimming. His skin was slightly pale, as if he was unaccustomed to being in the sun. His high, narrow face with symmetrical, angular cheekbones gave him a regal look. His slender nose and full masculine lips, made her wonder if they were as pillow soft as they looked. *Where the hell had that thought come from*? She swallowed, noting his strong, square jaw gave him a sense of strength and power. At first glance Julia would have guessed him to be in his late twenties, maybe early thirties.

Remembering to breathe, Julia sucked in a breath and realized she'd been staring like an idiot. Her gaze dropped to his rumpled, worn clothes. The shirt had most certainly seen better days. The dark blue and black, square-patterned shirt did nothing to hide the fact the man was built. He crossed his arms over his chest, and his arm muscles bunched. His tan pants were in even worse shape, but they clung to long, tree-stump sized legs. It was then she noticed he was barefoot.

Julia frowned. Her gaze made a return trip past those muscles and up to his six-foot four, maybe five, height. She met his gaze head on.

"Um, can I help you?" She didn't mean to sound breathy. She cleared her throat and drew in a deep, calming breath.

"You vorking."

A shiver skated down her spine at the sound of his deep, rich, slightly raspy voice, sounding like fine, matured wine. Julia realized his gaze was on her hands. She lifted them, showing her rubber gloves.

"Good guess." She gave him a half smile.

"I be vorking, too."

Easily, she picked up on his Russian accent but was confused by his words. He frowned. He seemed to be thinking.

"Lady, I Mohan. Look for vork. I vork for you. House need fix, da?"

Despite his drop dead gorgeous looks, the man had appeared to be living rough. Mohan. It was a strange name for a Russian. It sounded more Indian. She quickly glanced down at his feet again.

"Do you have any shoes?" she blurted out before she had thought better of it. He stiffened and unfolded his arms. She could see irritation in his expression. He seemed to be battling with himself.

"Need vork. Good at fix house. Buy shoes."

Emotions of uncertainty, mixed with compassion and tinted with a touch of fear, ran through her mind and body.

He needed to work; she needed a worker. It seemed rather odd he'd turn up the day after her arrival. Coincidence? Fate? Julia didn't know what it was. He was big and looked very strong--and a little scary.

"I um, I'm, there is a heck of a lot to do around here… I, um."

As she stumbled with her words, one of his regal black eyebrows rose in a curious manner.

"Vork hard for pretty lady." He gave her a half smile that could melt butter in the arctic. She felt her belly flutter. Hesitantly, she returned his smile.

One of her friends had once said, "Who cares what a man can or can't do? As long as he's hot eye candy… " Julia had thought it a shallow way to look at handsome buff men, but now she was starting to see her friend's point. She gazed over the majestic prince in rags standing proudly before her.

Instinct told Julia there was more to this man than just his youthful, striking good looks. She could see the bright intelligence behind his pale eyes and tense posture. Everything, even the twittering birds and laughing Kookaburras, fell silent. It was as if they too, along with Mohan, were waiting for her answer.

Her mother had told her she was crazy for leaving the city and her friends for a quiet, country life. She thought herself crazy for letting a large, dangerous tiger into her house--and liking the way it licked her breasts. Why not take the madness to a whole new level? She remembered her grandfather's old quote: *In for a penny, in for a pound.*

Julia gave him a welcoming smile and stepped away from the door to allow him access. Deep down, she knew she was inviting trouble, but in that moment, she didn't care. She silenced the voice of doubt in her brain. It was her life, damn it--not her mother's, not her ex-husband's, but her's. She could damn well do reckless things if she wanted to.

"Come on in, Mohan. I'm Julia. If you're good at fixing houses, then you've come to the right place. I'll make us a nice cuppa tea while we talk about what's to be done."

As she turned, she could see from the corner of her eye his chest exhaled and his tense shoulders relaxed. He ducked his head and followed her into the cottage.

Chapter Four

Julia was having trouble keeping her eyes off the big, tall, sexier-than-sin man in her house. She tripped on her camp chair and stumbled against her card table. Cups and plates came crashing down. Thankfully, the china did not break on the wooden floor.

"Sorry," she muttered, bending down to clear the mess.

Mohan crouched and scooped up several plates, setting them back on the table.

"You make tea, I clean."

She met his penetrating gaze then, without thought, she followed his order and stood up. Tea would certainly warm them up, and perhaps it would settle her stomach, which was determined to clench every time he looked at her.

"Um, okay," she replied, actually watching where she was going this time. She moved across to the kitchen bench where her camp stove and kettle were set up. She added more water, putting the kettle on to heat, before grabbing what she needed to make the tea.

"Is it rude of me to ask where you came from?"

"Siberia," he replied from behind her. That confirmed his Russian status. She turned around and saw he was leaning by the wall near the window, his arms folded, his gaze on the empty space on the floor near the fireplace. The mattress was no longer there, as she had put it back into the bedroom just after she'd dressed.

"I could tell you were Russian, but… "

"No, not Russia," he cut her off. "I am Siberia." From the venom in his tone, there was a clear difference.

"Okay, then--not Russian. What I meant was, where are you staying around this area? Most of this land beyond my property is the Australian National Park. Are you camping? Just visiting Australia?"

He was studying her as closely as she was studying him. She could almost see the thoughts moving through his brain, trying to pick out the right words to say.

"Camping. I visit Australia. Like this place very much."

Camping--without shoes and in worn clothes. Either something had happened to him, or he wasn't telling the truth.

Julia prickled at the thought. If there was one thing she hated, it was lies and deception. It was all she had ever been fed from her ex. She pursed her lips in annoyance.

The kettle boiled, and she took the moment to turn around. Making the tea gave her a chance to breathe. She realized her hands were shaking as she poured the boiling water into the mugs.

She never heard him move. Julia jumped out of her skin when his large hand settled over her own, removing the kettle from her grip.

She turned as he set the kettle down and had to tilt her head back to glare up at him.

"I won't stand being lied to." She did not care if she offended him or not. "I've put up with enough lies in my life, and I won't put up with them from you. Otherwise, you can go find work elsewhere."

~ * ~

She was smarter than he had given her credit for. A deep hurt hid behind her eyes. Her anger was justified, even though a good part of it was not wholly directed at him.

He liked the way she showed no fear as she stood up to him and made her position clear. He did not want to lie to her, but he couldn't fully trust her either.

He could at least try out part of his truth with her.

"Truth, Julia. I have vun avay from very bad men. I vas forced to jump from ship and svim very far. I valk to this safe mountain. Vhere I hide, I hunt to eat. I proud, vill not beg. I am good vorker. Build many house in my village. This is truth."

His hand still covered hers after he had set the kettle down. He curled his fingers around her hand and brought it to his chest to cover his pounding heart.

Anger drained from her eyes, replaced with…not pity--he would not be able to stand her looking at him with pity--but with a compassion he had not expected see. It moved him.

"I…I think I understand. You don't have to beg for anything, Mohan. I'll help you, and you'll help me."

And it would be in more ways than she realized.

With a smile he lifted her hand and placed a kiss on her knuckles. He watched as her pupils dilated and her breath quickened. Mohan released her hand and took a safe step back.

He struggled to reign in his reaction to this woman. Doubts flooded his mind. Perhaps his plan was not such a good idea. Mohan knew he had been in denial, only now he was coming to terms with the fact he was clearly attracted to her.

Keep a distance. Remain aloof. Be her worker or, at best, a friend. This was all he could offer.

The moment she licked her lips, he was forced to turn away. He was grateful when she returned to making the tea. Adding a generous amount of milk--he did like his milk--she lifted the mug to him. He took it from her hand and held it in salute to her.

"You're welcome," she said. He took pleasure in her small smile. "Do you have a place to sleep, Mohan?"

He gave her a nod. "*Da*, I have very good place. Am lucky to find nice lady. She give good bed, good food."

He watched as Julia's face turned down into another frown. If he wasn't mistaken, she was actually jealous. How curious.

"Hope it's an old lady," he heard her mutter just as she raised her mug to her lips.

He hid his sudden impish smile as he drank his own tea, savoring the milky flavour and rich aroma--and the heat he felt through his fingers. It was the first hot thing that had passed his lips in a long time.

If only she knew. But that was the whole point: She never would, if he could help it.

~ * ~

Problem was, not only did she now have an immigrant working for her, but Mohan was an illegal immigrant. If the authorities got wind of him being out here, he and she could get into deep trouble. Then there was the tiger. At least she assumed her tiger was Siberian also. Julia gave a snort of amusement as she guided her Rover into town, stopping out front of the hardware store.

It was ironic: her tiger was also an illegal immigrant. Wildlife goonies, and who knows who else, would be on her like a flash if they knew about the big cat stalking around her property. Good gracious, she hadn't been thinking this through. Her tiger would obviously hunt native animals: kangaroos, wallabies, possums, even koalas.

Perhaps if she fed him well enough and put a bell around his neck, it would help protect the wildlife.

Guilt ate at her. She hated lies and secrets. But to protect her new discoveries, she would have to keep her mouth shut. They were out of the way. No one need know about Mohan or her tiger.

He wasn't a housecat though. What she needed was information about white tigers--and a heck of a lot of meat.

She had left Mohan ripping out the bathroom pipes using tools from her ex's large toolkit. Equipment he had never used. Before she'd left to head into town, she had walked through the house, writing down a list of things he indicated he would need for each part of the house that warranted repair.

The store attendant was a youthful young man, with short cropped, sandy coloured hair, and a nametag stating *Matt* pinned over the left side of his chest on a red polo shirt.

"If you could have everything ready to go, I'll need to stop at the grocery store for supplies, too."

"Sure, no problem, lady. Any particular brand for the sander and floor polish?"

She smiled sweetly at the young attendant. "The best brand. Say, is there an internet café around here?"

"The café across the street has two computers. Hook ups a bit dodgy around here, but they got satellite. When you're ready," Matt added absently looking over her list again, "you can drive around back for the timber and pipes."

"Thanks!" She exited the store and walked across the street.

A café latte, a muffin, and ten minutes later Julia walked into the grocery store feeling anxious. From what she had discovered about white tigers, or any tigers in general, they ate up to forty pounds of meat per day.

She wondered if the average kangaroo weighed that much. She was going to attract attention buying that much meat from the supermarket. Perhaps she could find a local butcher or farmer to supply her with a steady stream of meat.

The tiger had seemed content with what she had given him the night before, but for his ongoing health, he would need more. Armed with a shopping trolley, she wandered up the aisle, adding various products to her cart. At the meat section, she cleared out the selection of pork and beef and added one tray of chicken for herself.

The wafting smell of cheap aftershave assaulted her nose; she glanced around to find John Leeman walking up behind her. The creepy Real Estate agent who had looked after her grandfather's property since his death. She'd only met the man once and instantly disliked him. His dark, thinning hair stood out against the gleaming white of his balding head. Small narrow eyes and a little nose seemed out of proportion with his overly large sized head.

She straightened as he walked passed and peered into her trolley. "Having a party, Mrs Cooper?" She tied not to wince at the sound of a nasally voice. He glanced up, his gaze on her breasts rather than her face as he talked.

Every inch of herself preservation screamed at her to be weary of this man, he'd already offered once to sell her grandfathers land, claiming to have ski resort buyers wanting to turn the area into a resort.

It would be a cold day in hell before she handed her land over to developers. The area surrounding her house was home to many other native plants and animals. They would have to bulldoze and destroy a hell of a lot of native forest in order to make a slope.

"You can never be stocked up on enough meat," she said smoothly meeting his brown gaze. "I'm having a freezer delivered tomorrow. I thought I'd prepare."

Julia wasn't lying, but she wasn't telling the entire truth either. It was none of his damn business what she was buying in the shops. "If you'll excuse me, I have to get back to the hardware store and collect the order waiting for me."

"I could make you three times what your property is really worth, Mrs Cooper. Resort developers are prepared to pay big bucks for that kind of land."

"Mr Leeman, I said I would think about it, but not the day after I have arrived. At any rate, I am here to stay for a good while."

He gave her a smile, which gave her the creeps. "Have dinner with me then. As you're new in town, let me welcome you properly."

Julia pursed her lips trying not to look disgusted by his invitation.

"That is nice of you, Mr Leeman, but no thank you. Right now all I want to focus on is getting my house in order. Maybe another time."

"I'll hold you to that," he said as she walked away.

Not if she could help it. A shudder ran down her spine.

Julia helped the girl at the checkout in order to hurry her purchases through. As she packed the food into bags, she ignored the clerk's raised eyebrow at all the meat.

Glad to be out of the grocery store, and with all the meat packed into her Rover, Julia hurried around to the hardware store.

Matt was waiting for her at the back entrance. He gave her a wave as she parked and opened her boot. She smiled back, and the young man started loading her goods. She wandered into the store where there were a few more items she wanted that hadn't been on her list. Thankfully, they had them in stock.

Chapter Five

Mohan was nowhere to be seen when she arrived back late in the afternoon. She had stopped at the post office to rent a post box and have all her mail redirected. The elderly lady behind the counter peppered her with questions. As soon Julia mentioned her grandfather, Mick Sheppard--the woman had known him--she kept Julia tied down with story after story.

As the post lady told her how much he had talked about Julia and her visits, about how much sadness he had expressed after her father had forbidden her to ever visit again, Julia struggled to keep the sorrow and tears at bay.

She had never known it was her father's decision. Why had he refused to let her go back to see her grandfather after that last visit on her seventh birthday? She never fully understood what had happened between her mother and her grandfather.

Carrying an armful of supplies, Julia nudged open the door with her hip. She found everything in the main living area untouched. She dumped her first load of meat onto the counter and wandered through the house. She gasped to see the floorboards of her bedroom cleaned and the bed assembled, including the mattress. The bathroom had also been stripped bare, with the old tub gone. It was too rusted out to use at any rate. That was something else she would need to order. But the toilet, which had been thoroughly cleaned, was still there and seemed in good working order.

She gave a squeal of glee when it flushed and refilled. No more going outside to visit the outhouse. Mohan was not just a good worker but a great handyman.

With a resigned sigh, she assumed Mohan had gone back to his lodgings. As she pondered where he could be staying, she filled the kettle from the tap and set it on to boil. Then she proceeded to unpack the Rover. She heated three kettles in succession and filled two buckets with warm water. She shoved as much meat as she could into the icebox before placing the rest into a stainless steel bowl she had bought from the hardware store. She left the piled meat just outside the front door, hoping to bring her tiger back.

With a towel slung over her shoulder, she grabbed her clothes and toiletries. Picking up the steaming buckets of water with her free hand, she went outside by the back shed to have a sponge bath.

The hot water system, gas cylinders, refrigerator, and generator would not arrive until the next day. She had not had a shower since the previous morning, and she was feeling grimy from the housecleaning. Now it was time to clean herself.

~ * ~

Mohan lay along the line of trees feeling warmer than he had in a long time. The sun heated his fur, and he rolled and stretched. The satisfaction of a hard day's labour was not wasted on him.

He had seen Julia's vehicle return to the house. His mouth watered from smelling the meat she had bought and laid out for him. His meal would not be had for free--he would work harder to earn his keep and guard her by night.

His keen eyes caught sight of her moving around to the back of the house burdened with buckets of steaming water. She set the water down and placed her clothes and towel on the flat head of the corner post.

He rolled over and sat up, mesmerized as she began to strip off her clothes. Mohan understood she was about to bathe. He had seen her naked the night before, but in the full sunlight, she was even more breathtaking. Her breasts a creamy pale, so soft and full. Her nipples the size of coins, dark pink with their rigid peaks tight in the cool mountain breeze. Even from the distant place where he sat, he could see her skin pebble with goose bumps. Remembering how tantalizing she had tasted, Mohan realized he was purring. Even in tiger form, pure wanton lust surged through him.

Her tummy was rounded, giving way to full, soft hips and a curved ass that any sane, red-blooded man would kill to possess. The triangular thatch of curls at the junction of her thighs--auburn like the curls hanging free around her shoulders--had him purring louder. She lifted the soaked sponge and let the water trickle down her lush body. All sensibility of thought abandoned him. Acting on pure instinct, he rose on all fours and began stalking his prey.

~ * ~

Julia lifted her foot, placing it on the lower wooden fence rail as she smoothed the lotion over it and scrubbed it clean. She dunked the sponge back into the bucket and proceeded to wash off the soap. Despite the warm sun, the cool air was making her skin prickle. She hurried her movements making sure she had her entire body clean before starting on her hair.

She never saw him coming. A big fury body knocked her sideways. Air whooshed from her lungs. She had landed heavily on the soft wet grass. Twisting her body in the grass, she found a big paw placed on the center of her chest, just below her breasts. She was pinned under the huge growling tiger.

The sudden panic she was about to be eaten vanished as the beast ducked his head, his long pink tongue darted out, and began licking the water off her skin starting in the valley between her breasts.

Julia's breathing became hard and fast as he found her breasts again, licking her with a savoring slowness. It stole her breath.

She squeaked, not knowing what to do to dislodge the big tiger as he shifted and his tongue licked lower. He followed each rivulet of water on her body as he moved dangerously low. Her stomach clenched as his tongue pushed into her belly button. Her skin pebbled with sensation, and she fought back a moan.

She was getting a cat bath, and it was turning her on. *Oh, no, no, no.* This was not right.

"Don't you dare go any further, Mister!" She had intended to yell, but it came out more of a breathy pant as she squirmed under the tiger's relentless tongue.

She gripped the tiger's head and pushed with all the strength she could muster. He seemed to get the message and removed his paw. The big cat took a step back and gazed at her with hooded tiger eyes. His pink tongue flicked out to lick his chops.

Julia made her escape. Rolling onto her stomach, she pushed to her hands and knees and grabbed for the towel hanging over the fence rail. It was just out of reach.

A squeal pierced the air as her tiger's wet nose shoved right in between her ass cheeks. His tongue speared forward through the folds of her sex.

She toppled forward, falling with a yelp onto her upper arms. He growled low and deep.

Shock rolled through her as his abrasive tongue touched her clit, sliding all the way back up to her ass. The sensation was unlike anything she had ever felt. He nuzzled in and attacked again, swiping with hurried laps of his tongue. Its roughness dragged against her sensitive flesh sending spikes of pleasure through her.

She forced her mind to start working again. For god's sake, she was being molested by a tiger! What was worse, she was enjoying it!

"Damn it, Mo! Stop that right now! I am not a tiger or a cat." Julia gripped the rail tightly and pulled herself up and away from the tiger. She ripped the towel off the fence and quickly wrapped it around her body. Her chest heaved with the effort to breath.

The tiger sat back on his hunches, staring at her. He licked his lips as if he couldn't wait to get another taste.

"This is not going to work if you keep doing that! You must have been one heck of a pet if they trained you to think people are cats, or maybe you think you're people."

The tiger blinked, once again giving her a dry stare. He turned and casually walked back towards the house, leapt up onto the porch, and proceeded to eat the meat dinner.

Julia glanced down at her body. She was a mess, with wet grass plastered all over her. There was also no way in hell she was getting undressed again with a perverse tiger running around.

With trembling fingers, she grabbed her clothes and walked back to the house on shaky legs. She was trying damn hard to ignore the heat in her belly and the ache between her thighs.

"This is sooo wrong," she muttered, eyeing the tiger as he devoured the raw pork roasts. She slammed the door of the house. She would finish her bath in the house with cold water, standing on her towels.

Mo. It was only after she had managed to cool her body down then dressed in a warm T-shirt and thick jumper, with equally thick denim jeans that she remembered the name that had slipped out. Mo. It was a perfect name for her rude Siberian tiger.

Outside, it had grown dark and cold. The tiger still sat by the door. Not wanting him to feel cold, she opened it and the tiger raised his head to regard her.

"You're only allowed in on one condition: You keep that tongue in your mouth and away from any part of my skin that isn't a hand or my face! Got that?"

He purred loudly as he rubbed his big furry body against hers, striding past her and into the house. As he settled by the fire, it occurred to her maybe she hadn't just adopted a big dangerous cat--he had adopted her.

She shook the silly thought from her mind and closed the door. Her stomach groaned in complaint. She had missed lunch.

"This is all your fault," she informed her tiger. "You made me skip my lunch. While buying food for you, I had the creepy real estate agent corner me in the supermarket. It's bad enough he can't keep his eyes off my breasts. I come home to have a three hundred pound tiger pouncing on me. It's enough to drive anyone to the brink of insanity."

Dicing up some chicken breast with a sharp knife, she added it to a heating pan. "Well, at least I'm glad you weren't here when Mohan turned up. You would have scared the poor man away. That's why I'm going to call you Mo. After all, it doesn't take a genius to figure out you're both from the same place. I wonder why you both seem to have the same remarkable eyes."

Julia thought about her words for a moment. "I wonder if Mohan knows anything about tigers. All I got was some info off the Internet telling me you eat up to forty pounds of meat a day. I mean, forty pounds!

That's a quarter of my body weight every day. Just what were you living on before I arrived?"

Of course, the tiger just continued to stare at her. She added some pre-sliced vegetables and a bit of seasoning to her sizzling pan to complete her dinner.

"Apart from you, Mo, I've never met a man so… " She plated her chicken stir fry and sat down in her camp chair facing the fire and Mo. "…so deep, intense, and sexy, all rolled into one. Granted, his English isn't very good. Not that it matters. Now, why couldn't I have met a man like that before Richard? I bet he knows how to treat a woman and not run around chasing every other woman in the city."

She popped a piece of tender chicken into her mouth and chewed thoughtfully. "I can't begin to imagine what kind of life he had before jumping ship. I wonder what he meant by bad people. I'm all for minding my own business, but I hate lies. My ex-husband was the smoothest liar I've ever known. Stupid me. I fell for them over and over again." Anger made her stomach clench, and she lost her appetite. Julia sighed and set her plate aside.

"Maybe I'm doing this all wrong, running away to the country instead of living it up in the city. I've got money. Why shouldn't I go find some hot man to have some hot sex with?" Julia shook her head. Richard had been the only lover she had ever had.

"I feel like I've wasted half my life, and what do I do? Go run and hide. I'm a mess, Mo. You may not want an owner who's all messed up."

The tiger got up from his fireside spot and rubbed against her legs. Julia, comforted by her big cat, slipped off the camp chair and sank to her knees. She slid her arms around his neck, hugging the beast tightly against her. His loud purr vibrated through her body. "Damn it, Mo," she said softly. "I really wish you weren't a tiger. You've got a hell of a wicked tongue on you." Julia chuckled. "But I love your company just as much."

Mo pulled back and gave her face a swipe with his tongue. Julia giggled. "Behave now, or you'll be sleeping outside."

~ * ~

She had left him to sleep by the fire. With his acute hearing, he knew when her breathing evened out and she had fallen into deep slumber. Mohan shifted and opened her bedroom door. He gazed down at her sleeping form. She was relaxed peaceful. Several strands of Julia's hair had fallen across her face. He reached out his hand and brushed back the wayward tresses.

The more he observed her--the slight dusting of freckles across the bridge of her nose, the little dip in her chin line, the soft, rounded cheeks, and elegant, high cheekbones--the more beautiful she grew.

So many things drew him to her, even against his will. She was a mixture of so many qualities: strength and stubbornness, vulnerability and a deeply caring heart. The little speeches she made to him in his tiger form revealed much more than she would have shown him while in his human form.

He wanted to tear out the heart of this man who had hurt her. She deserved someone to care for her, to love her body as it was made to be loved.

She had proven just how much power she had over him by making him lose his head over the sight of her naked and bathing. The sound of her voice scolding him as she desperately tried to escape his paws and tongue had shaken him out of his lust-drenched stupor. He saw exactly what he was doing--something he should never have done.

He was angry with himself for his loss of control. It was dangerous and stupid. The taste of her skin and, most especially, the taste of her arousal refused to leave him--even after he had eaten the pig meat and finished off her small meal of chicken.

Yet, there was more. She warmed him. The coldness of his despair and loneliness was eased in her presence. Her beauty radiated when she smiled. He cherished her touch and the way her fingers curled through his fur. He smiled, remembering the dazed look she gave him in his man form. The warmth of her body next to his while they slept gave him a sense of belonging.

Again he battled with himself. Why was he finding it so hard to control his urges around her? The smart, sensible thing to do was to leave her bedroom, leave her to sleep. Mohan shifted and leapt onto the bed, stretching out beside her. She turned in her sleep, and her fingers reached for him and slid though his fur. He could do nothing but purr in contentment. He did not want to give up his newfound warmth and comfort just yet. He would simply need to make sure he was not around when she undressed. He had to tread with more care, be more watchful and vigilant. He wanted to protect her, even from himself.

Chapter Six

Hammering woke Julia. She bolted upright in bed and blinked rapidly against the light streaming in the window. That's odd, she thought. She could have sworn Mo had slept next to her during the night. She glanced at the door. Unless her tiger had grown opposable thumbs, though, there was no way he could have.

So where was her big pet? She realized it was Mohan hammering, fixing the hole in the roof of the spare bedroom. He must have found the ladder and supplies he had requested.

Julia grabbed her dark red satin robe, which hung over the end of her bed. The bare wooden floors were cold on her feet. She made a mental note to buy rugs next time she went shopping.

Mo was not anywhere to be found. Mohan must have let him out. Her eyes widened with the thought. She yanked open the door. Blinking against the bright sunshine, she glanced up at the roof. He sat perched near the edge, hammering slats into place.

"Good morning, Mohan."

He paused and glanced down at her. Her heart hammered in her chest when he lifted his hammer, giving her a wave and a breathtaking smile. "You, um, haven't seen a… " What? Big white tiger? He would think her mad.

He was waiting for her to finish her question. "Um, never mind. Would you like some tea?"

"I finish roof, then come for tea," he replied gruffly.

"Okay." Julia went back inside to dress and put on the kettle to boil. Mohan continued to hammer away rhythmically.

She was still puzzling over her tiger. With her feet in warm socks and sneakers, she poured the boiling water into the mugs and dunked the teabags before adding the milk. She had noticed Mohan liked his tea with lots of milk. She rummaged through her dry supplies for a packet of sweet biscuits. Not the healthiest breakfast in the world, but she did not care as she bit into the sugary cookie and quickly devoured the treat.

Not long after, the hammering ceased, and Mohan opened the door. She turned with a smile. "Come on in. Sit down. It must be freezing up on my roof."

"No mind dis cold. Dis not cold. Siberia very cold." He took the mug she offered and lowered his large frame into the camp chair. It groaned under his weight.

"I can only imagine how cold your country is. It snows up here in winter. I don't know how long you've been out here, but to me, it's cold enough." She rubbed her arms at the thought of the coming snow.

Julia left her steaming cup on the counter, snatched the big white shopping bag, and held it out to him.

"These are for you. I'm very good at judging people's sizes. I worked in a plus-size clothing store for three years."

He set aside his mug and gently took the bag from her hands. He pulled out a shirt, large jumper, and black denim working jeans, along with several pairs of thick socks. With a smile, she fetched the box by the side of the door and opened it to reveal a sturdy pair of Warragul work boots.

Mohan laid the clothes in his lap and took the boots. She could see he was trying to hide his trembling hands as he gripped the shoebox.

"I vill vork very hard, pay for these."

Julia gave him a kind smile. "No, these are a gift from me."

He simply stared at her as if he did not know what to say or how to react.

"It is customary in Australia to at least say 'Thank you' for a gift."

He swallowed, struggling with some emotion which she had trouble identifying. Was he angry at her for buying him clothes?

Worry consumed her over his reaction. "I didn't mean to offend you. If you feel you can't accept a gift from me… " She drew in a breath and turned away.

Mohan caught her wrist. His touch sent an electric jolt of awareness through her body. He set the clothes down and rose to his feet, towering above her. She stared up into his pale blue eyes intense with emotion. Julia suddenly found herself crushed in a tight embrace.

"Thank you, Julia," he rumbled.

She felt his move with each breath. His arms were strong, holding her so tightly she could hardly breathe. Just as suddenly, he released her and stepped back.

Julia did not have a clue what was going on in his head. Why would a simple gift of clothes move him and make him clamp down at the same time? Wasn't he used to receiving presents? It was the only explanation she could come up with.

"I've got a heap of stuff being delivered today. We'll have power once the generator is installed, and a water heater running on gas. It should make life and work a bit easier."

She hoped taking the focus off her gift would make him feel more comfortable. "I want to go back into town. I saw a bathtub and vanity unit at the big hardware store. I'm sure they'll deliver that too. I don't want to take sponge baths outside anymore."

Mohan, who had set aside his new clothes and reached for his tea, suddenly spluttered out the liquid. He gave a cough before drawing in a deep breath.

"Um, you okay?" She had moved quickly around to pat him firmly on the back. There was a look in his eye she could not quite place.

"Da, tis good, I go back to vork now." He stood quickly, knocking the chair backwards. Julia jumped out of the way to avoid it crashing onto her feet. He scooped up his clothes and hastily exited the house.

Julia stared at the open door. She wondered what the heck was going on with Mohan. So many things puzzled her about him. Mind you, she barely knew the man. She knew the old expression *curiosity killed the cat*, but heck, she was very curious about this handsome Siberian man--and not all of her curiosity was about his past life or what was going on in his mind.

~ * ~

He made himself scarce as soon as he first heard the rumbling trucks coming up the dirt track. Sitting out of sight on a large fallen tree, he set down the clothes she'd given him and stared at them.

It felt strange. Mohan wasn't sure he liked the sentiment her gifts had evoked in him. He was more than grateful; they were something he needed. He also felt obliged to do or give her something in return. At the same time, he was giddy with a sense of elation he had never before felt.

He was just so used to fighting and working hard to obtain everything he ever had.

Anger poured through him as he remembered his small village, hidden away from the world in order to protect their secret; the curse that made them what they were. Magic? Mohan did not know about that, but it had always set them apart from the others. Any who did know about them feared them, thought them unnatural, freakish.

Even keeping away from the thrum of the world had not been enough--not enough to protect any of his people. In the span of a heartbeat, they had surrounded the village, outnumbering his people with superior firepower.

Mohan tore at his old clothes and shifted. He leapt over an old fallen tree in one powerful bound. What could he have done to save them? Why had he not fought harder? Birds and native animals scattered as he ran, hard and fast; ran until his heart thundered painfully against the ribs in his chest not caring if the thick undergrowth of the forest scratched his skin or tore his fur.

Guilt swamped over him for taking comfort in this land, in Julia, in the gifts she had bestowed on him. He needed to feel the pain again. He didn't want to forget what had happened. He needed to suffer as they had.

He let out a mighty anguished roar as he came to a halt by a stream. He collapsed into the water, panting for breath.

Dizzy and unfocused, he slowly dragged himself onto his paws and began making his way back through the forest, back to her. It was a dangerous thing to need something or someone; he knew it only brought more pain. There were many doubts and fears eating at him. What if they found him? What if he could not protect her as he had been unable to protect his family? What had he to give her? Even with all this in mind, he was unable to stop himself. He couldn't understand how one human woman could affect him so deeply. What was it about her that kept drawing him back? He had wanted to be in control, and around her, he had anything but.

~ * ~

Julia was miffed Mohan hadn't returned after the trucks had gone. She was forced to use her checkbook for bribes--to bribe the generator deliveryman to hook up the power for her, to bribe the water heater man to properly install the system near the bathroom at the back of the house. It still needed pipes Mohan was supposed to install after the men had gone.

Where was he? She stood on the porch, scanning the surrounding forest. He had taken the clothes and boots she had given him. Maybe he was one of those immigrants out to use her for what he could get. But no, she may not know him that well, but he stood proudly. Somehow, deep down, she knew he would not do a thing like that.

The single roar coming from the forest made her heart pound in sudden fear. Mo! Something was wrong. She pushed her thoughts about Mohan aside and ran down the steps. She headed into the forest to begin franticly searching for her big white cat.

In the distance, she spied the white tiger among the dark green forest undergrowth, walking almost drunkenly towards her. Closing the distance between them, Julia stopped short when she saw the state of his beautiful white and black coat. Parts of his body were matted in blood.

"Good gracious, Mo! What have you been up to?"

Breathless from running, she dropped to her knees and wrapped her arms around his neck, hugging his big body close to hers. She could feel the big feline trembling in her grip. "Oh, beautiful boy. If you weren't way too big for me to carry back to the house, I would. Come on, let's go home. I'll make you a big warm bowl of milk and honey, make it feel all better."

She was wondering if there was more wrong with Mo than just his cuts--and if she would need to call a vet. She swallowed her concern. Bringing a vet into the equation would alert the authorities to a tiger on her property.

She let go of his neck and rose to her feet. He nuzzled into the back of her legs before walking placidly by her side all the way back to the house.

Once inside, she threw her sleeping bag down, unsure how to treat the bleeding wounds.

"I'm going to get a bowl of warm water and wash these cuts, just don't bite my head off for helping you, okay?" she said gently as he lay down by the fire, his wide, pale blue eyes watching her all the while.

She prepared a bowl of water and sat beside him, washing every scratch she could find through the thick fur. Not once did he growl or show any indication of pain, apart from the twitching and swishing of his tail. His purr, once she'd finished, made her sigh in relief.

"I have no idea what you get up to during the day, and it's starting to worry me."

She sat back, folding her legs as she stroked him from the top of his head down along his back. "I'm worried I'm not feeding you the right amount. Worried you're going to get spotted and taken from me."

As if trying to give her some comfort, Mo shifted and laid his big head into her lap.

"Despite your tendency to have a wayward tongue, how could I not love a creature as beautiful and majestic as you?" she confessed to the purring tiger.

He rose up and licked her face, making her giggle as she tried to shove him away.

"Okay, okay! Well, I've got to figure out a way to keep you out of trouble so I can keep you--that is, if you want to keep me to."

She laughed again as he nuzzled into her chest, purring loudly. "I'll take that as a yes then."

Chapter Seven

He had not even knocked. Julia groaned and rolled out of bed, sighing when she noticed Mo had gone again. How he got out was a complete mystery to her. She thought it best not to think too hard on it, or she would develop a headache.

She had spent the afternoon sanding down the floor in the spare room. Mo had slept by the fire. He woke once to wolf down a large platter of meat and lap up all the sweetened milk, while she had her soup and toast. Afterward, he had followed her into her bedroom and plonked himself down on the left side of the bed. He never opened his eyes as she got ready for bed.

The timber in the spare room was still good. All it needed now was a good lick of floor varnish. The window still needed replacing, though, but one job at a time. If it weren't for Mohan, she would have barely anything finished.

But here he was, just after six am, hammering away at the pipes in her bathroom. Still in her pjs, she wandered in and leaned against the doorframe. He was dressed in his new clothes and had the new boots on as he worked, measuring the metal piping before vigorously cutting it to length with the hacksaw.

"We have power now. You can use the mitre saw on those."

Mohan swung around and straightened his tall frame. Julia noticed right away he had a small red cut on the side of his face and another on the back of his hand. She drew in a sharp breath as his heated gaze swept over her from head to toe, as if any moment he would pounce and ravish her.

She blinked, and the look had vanished. Had she just imagined Mohan's look of sudden, raw, sexual interest? She was still annoyed over his disappearing act the day before.

"Good to vork muscle, stay strong." He gave her a small smile.

Damn it, what was it with this man that sent her world off kilter? Despite his being drop-dead gorgeous, it took just a word or a smile from him and any anger evaporated.

"I was worried about you yesterday when you didn't come back. Are you okay?"

"Da, good. Needed...vot is vord? Make head right."

"Needed time to clear your head," she translated.

He nodded. "You go get bath. I fix pipes."

"After breakfast I will. I need my cup of tea to wake up. Make you one too?"

"Da, Julia make good tea. Much milk." He grinned again, and her heart literally skipped a beat.

"Have you eaten? I have a hankering for some scrambled eggs. After all, I need some protein since my cat has been eating all my meat," she said without thinking.

"He no need so much."

Mohan's comment left her blinking in surprise. Her stomach pitched in sudden fear. The cut on his hand and the one on his face--it occurred to her that he may have had an encounter with Mo.

She stood up straight. "Um…what do you know about my cat?"

Mohan gave a knowing grin. "Big Siberian tiger. Like me, from Siberia. He no eats so much. He likes lady very much."

Relief made her feel almost giddy. She had a small chuckle. Mohan did know about Mo. More importantly, he knew about caring for tigers.

"Thank god for that. I was beginning to worry…"

"Julia vorry too much. Mo no trouble to you. I no trouble to you."

"So you know what he does all day?"

"He big cat. All cat like sleep in sunshine. Like roll in vater, in leafs. Come home for big food, grow lazy, fat on beautiful Julia's food."

She gave a laugh, and Mohan smiled. "I'm glad to hear that. I'll go make us those eggs then. I am almost dying for a real hot water shower or bath."

She grinned and headed for her makeshift kitchen, more than happy to be preparing a meal for two again.

~ * ~

John Leeman sat in front of his computer, staring at an image of Julia Cooper. The photo had been taken at someone's party, posted on one of her friend's Facebook pages.

He had managed to dig up quite a bit on the newly divorced woman, but nothing he could use to his advantage. What held his interest most of all was the court settlement from her divorce--it had left her a wealthy woman.

From small media and business articles, he learned her father had owned a large export company, which her ex-husband now ran. But apparently Julia still had a controlling hand in it. Over ninety percent of the shares belonged to her.

Her poor ex-husband could not even sneeze on company grounds without her say so.

He had a fixation for large breasted women, and even more so for large breasted women with money. The stupid woman was also sitting on a developer's goldmine. He had tried to tell her about the value of her land. Typical stubborn, stupid, woman: she would not listen.

Opportunity had walked into his office in the form of the plump, auburn-haired woman. His currently mounting debt was one that needed to be paid, but all his available funds were strictly in use for his little habit. He took pleasure in the thrill of a well-placed bet here and there, and sometimes the investment returned big. Sometimes you lucked out and sometimes you lost.

Julia Cooper was a good bet, and one he was going to invest in to gain rich rewards.

If he could get Julia to date him--even marry him--not only would it be a huge step up from where he sat now, but with his debts cleared, he could indulge even more in his favorite pastime.

He had only made one attempt to invite her to dinner. She had scampered away like a startled rabbit. It didn't mean he would give up just yet.

John clicked his computer mouse and easily accessed the satellite the café across the street used for its wireless Internet. He already knew all the passwords needed to remotely access their computers.

He knew Mrs Cooper had been in there using a computer, so he went back through the browser history to find just what she had been up to.

She had checked her e-mail: just a few messages from Melbourne friends, one from her mother, and another from her solicitor. Her second task was much more curious. She had spent quite a bit of time researching white tigers. He followed the same links she had.

Why would she want to know how much tigers ate and how to care for them? Did she have an exotic pet? All the meat in her shopping trolley would certainly support the thought.

Grasping at straws? Maybe, but it certainly warranted investigation.

He considered the current facts before him: rich woman, divorced and living alone. She would need a sympathetic ear, someone she could complain to about her ex-husband. She would need a shoulder to cry on.

He shifted, pulling his wallet from his pocket and flipping it open. He had plenty to buy her some flowers. But then again, his neighbour, Mrs Milligan, always had plenty of roses in her garden. She would not notice a few missing blooms. He would use his funds to buy some cheap wine.

Soon he would pay the solitary Mrs Cooper a visit.

Chapter Eight

She was fantasizing again. For two days she had been slipping into daydreams of Mohan. It was hard to stay focused whenever he was near. She was certain she had caught him staring at her with that same raw hunger she had noticed the first time in the bathroom.

Every time they worked in the same room, touched or even shared a laugh, her stomach clenched and moisture pooled between her thighs. Every time she brought him a cup of tea, his fingers brushing hers as he took the mug from her hands, her skin heated and her nipples tightened with need. She was going insane with lust over the guy.

On the third day, she was almost out of her mind. She worked with extra vigor, trying to suppress her newfound sexual hunger, trying to go over in her head why she should not lust after him. One, he was younger than her. Two, he worked for her--everyone knew you should never mix business with pleasure. And three…she was trying to think of a third reason when Mohan appeared at the open door. She had been putting the last coat of floor varnish onto the spare room's floor. It was her aim to move into this room and start on the main bedroom.

"Julia, come." He gave her a mischievous smile. Her heart hammered against her ribcage, and her belly clenched. Damn it, she was wet between her thighs. There was hardly a time when Julia was not aroused just by thinking about Mohan. Thank god for thick jeans, she thought dryly.

She set down her brush and climbed to her feet. He held out his hand to her, and, without hesitation, she placed hers into his. Warm tingles spread through her arm, right through her body.

Mohan drew her out into the hall and spun her around, unexpectedly placing himself behind her with his large hands over her eyes.

Julia's breath quickened with the mixed combination of Mohan's hands on her face and the fact she could not see a thing.

"Mohan?"

"Valk, I have surprise."

She let him walk her forward a few feet. Then he turned her and stopped. She knew the layout of the old place well enough to know he'd just taken her into the bathroom.

Light flooded her eyes as he removed his hands. She blinked rapidly, readjusting to the brightness. She gasped, staring at her new, gleaming white bathroom; complete with a bathtub and a vanity unit. All the shiny silver taps were in place along with the showerhead hanging over the bath. The translucent, white shower curtain she had bought was hung up and swept to one side.

He leaned over turning on the shower tap. Within a few moments, she saw the steam from hot water rising.

Julia squealed with utter delight.

"Mohan, you are a genius! This is perfect!" Without thinking, she jumped into his arms and placed kisses all over his face. His arms stole about her waist.

She stilled suddenly, realizing he had stiffened. She met his intense gaze, their lips so close to each other she couldn't stand it any longer. She wanted to kiss him. All her sexual frustrations from the past few days came crashing down on her. She rose onto her tiptoes, and pressed her lips to his.

His arms tightened around her, almost crushing her against him as she nibbled and sucked on his lips. She gave a soft moan as she ran her tongue over the seam of his lips.

He beat her to it. His mouth opened over hers, suddenly responding hungrily and taking control of the kiss with a fervour that stole her breath.

He gave a sudden groan; a low growl came from his throat. Julia found herself torn from his lips and arms as Mohan shoved her roughly back from him. He was panting, his hand clearly trembling. He was shaking his head, not looking at her.

"No, not my kind," he said clear as day.

Like a sharp lash, his words cut through her deeply. She swallowed, feeling suddenly mortified at what she had done.

"Oh, god! I'm…I'm so sorry," she choked on a sudden sob.

He raised his head and anger blazed in his eyes.

Needing to be anywhere else but here in this moment, Julia spun on her heels and ran from the house and kept running.

Damn it, why had she done that? Why had she kissed him like a stupid, desperate, woman? Because she was a stupid, desperate, woman!

"He's younger than you, and now he hates you," she scolded herself, stomping through the bushland, making no observation of where she was going.

She had been wrong, seeing something in his eyes that was not really there. His reaction, the way he had pushed her away, had hurt her more than his rejection. *Not his kind.* The words still vibrated angrily through her mind.

"Stupid, stupid, stupid! I'm nothing but a stupid idiot--and he's a bigot."

Richard was right. She was a stupid, fat, frigid bitch. Julia's vision blurred as tears escaped her eyes and began streaming unendingly down her cheeks.

Everything had come to a boiling point. Richard, her mother, the divorce--and now she was alone. For too long all of her bad feelings and emotions had been stamped down and bottled up. Mohan's words and actions were the final catalyst to make everything shatter.

Julia, blinded by her tears, stumbled on a rock. She cried out as her ankle twisted, falling heavily onto leafy ground. She threw back her head and screamed her frustrations mixed with the sudden pain shooting through her leg. Slumped down on the leafy floor, she sobbed her heart out.

"Julia! Julia!"

From where he had come, she had no idea, but Mohan's worried face was hovering over her, his big hands were lifting her, touching her.

"No, don't touch me." She fought him as he pulled her into his strong arms and held her tightly against his hard chest. She lost the battle and sobbed into his shirt.

He rocked her in his arms like a child until her sobs subsided. She felt comforted, but she also felt awkward. She didn't know what to say to him or how to excuse her behavior.

"Ve are… " Mohan's voice was gentle, "…much alike. Ve have deep vound, inside heart."

Julia swallowed and drew in a shuddering breath before she spoke. "I'm sorry I tried to kiss you."

She felt his chest rumble with a chuckle. "I push avay because I know, if I kiss you, I vill not stop. You are very beautiful voman. You tempt beyond control."

She was surprised by this, but still, there was reality to face. "It shouldn't have happened anyway. I'm much older and should know better."

He moved his arm, slipping his hand under her chin and raising it. He forced her to meet his clear blue depths. With the pad of his thumb, he wiped the wet path of her tears.

"I much older than looks, Julia." His lips were but a whisper away from hers. "Tell me no, Julia, and I vill stop."

She could feel his whole body trembling, as if he was trying to restrain himself.

Selfishly, she didn't want him to. She wanted all that was Mohan. She shut out the part of her brain that told her this was wrong. Here in his arms, it felt good, right. Julia pushed herself up and met his lips with hers.

Unlike before, Mohan did not bother to contain the raw hunger she had seen in his gaze. He gripped the back of her head and took firm control of both her and their kiss.

His tongue speared into hers, stroking, possessing every recess of her mouth, before sucking her tongue back into his own mouth. Oh god, she never realized a kiss could be like this: so hot and carnal.

Julia enjoyed sex even if she did not come every time with Richard. Sex had been an infrequent pleasure in her life. Richard had been too busy, out and about, pleasuring every other woman but her.

The heat curling through her made her feel wanton and desperate. Something needed to be done to ease the ache. The man devouring her mouth was the man she needed.

Recklessly, she met his wild kiss and felt equally wild as he pushed her back onto the ground, covering her with his warm body. His hands groped at her clothes in a desperation she mirrored.

Her efforts seemed hampered, but it appeared he had no difficulty in rendering her naked. Her T-shirt was torn from her torso, and he made short work of her bra. He let her breathe as he gripped the waistband of her jeans and ripped them down her legs, her shoes coming off in the single sweep. She ignored the pain of her ankle as he pounced onto her and placed himself between her open thighs.

She could feel the hardness of his length pressing into her inner thigh.

A low growl emanated from his throat, reminding her very much of Mo, but the thought fled from her mind as he left a wet trail of open-mouthed kisses over chin and onto her throat. He lingered at the juncture between her neck and shoulder. He sucked down hard on her flesh, making her cry out and moan as it sent a spike right through her body, driving her into a sexual frenzy of pure wanton need. She arched her back, trying to wrap her legs around him and push her sex against his leg, unashamedly trying to dry hump him, seeking what she needed.

He growled again, pushing her hips flat onto the ground, and attached his mouth to her right breast. He sucked hard and ran his tongue over the engorged bud--just like her tiger had done. He then attacked the other with as much devoted yet hurried attention.

Julia was beyond ready to have him.

"Hurry, Mohan, I want you inside me," she pleaded, quite willing to beg for what she wanted. As he pushed her thighs wide and aligned their lower bodies, she realized she had no idea when he had rid himself of his pants. She felt the thick head of his cock push through her fold and connect with the mouth of her sex. Julia arched her hips, and the first inch slipped into her.

~ * ~

Mohan moaned, pleasure enveloping him as he slid into the wet heat of Julia's hot tight channel.

His little wildcat was clawing at his back, her legs around his hips, as he withdrew and plunged in again, trying to relive that first moment of connection. What he got was even better: the friction of their bodies sparking wave after wave of hedonistic pleasure. Mohan drove after the delight, chasing it with each thrust, trying to push deeper, as if he could touch her soul with his body.

Julia arched her back, panting, her head thrown back, her eyes closed. He understood her eager pursuit of the pleasure and the passion.

Mohan fell on her, holding her tightly to him as he pushed them both to the pinnacle he knew was coming. Her body began to tremble under his. He wanted her completion, needed her satisfaction. It was the only thing driving his.

Julia's scream ripped through the forest. She panted his name over and over as she shuddered. Her walls clenching around his driving cock were enough to push him over the edge. It burst unexpectedly through his body, and he let out a wail as his body jerked and his seed emptied deeply into Julia's body.

She had proven to him he was not as numb and cold as he had believed. Julia was a bright flame chasing away his darkness and cold.

He did not understand it, but, for once, he did not want to understand, only to touch and to feel. She strengthened his heart, giving him a new hope.

They both had deep inner wounds and, perhaps, it was fate they had found each other. He did not know about himself, but he would try and help heal this fragile woman's wounds the best he could, just as she was starting to heal his.

Chapter Nine

He had not even taken off his shirt, and yet here she was completely naked. She felt a little miffed he only pushed down his pants. He pulled them up again before she could glimpse of any part of his naked flesh--bare hands and feet aside. Then again, in the aftermath of the best sex she had ever had on the mossy, leafy ground of a forest, who was she to complain?

"You are hurt." His large warm hands skimmed down her leg, reaching her ankle. She winced when he applied pressure.

"I fell," she mumbled not sure how to feel or act after such desperate sex. Mohan glanced up to meet her gaze. His smile eased the discomfort. He gently touched the side of her face.

"You no valk. I carry."

Even before she could protest, he placed an arm under her knees and shoulders and graccfully rose to his feet.

"Mohan, I'm too damn heavy to carry," she finally managed to inform him, after being both stunned and impressed by his show of strength.

"Shush. No heavy. I carry, easy."

"Did you just shush me?" She anchored her arms around his neck, feeling indignant as he strode purposefully back towards the house.

"You have much vind."

Julia blinked in confusion at his words. "Vind? You mean wind?"

She could see him thinking through his words again.

"Vind, talk much to say no."

She did not know whether to be insulted or not.

"I think you're trying to tell me I'm long winded," she said dryly.

An impish smile spread across his face, making her heart gather speed once again. Mohan was too sexy for his own good--for *her* own good! Look what it had gotten her: a most likely sprained ankle and an orgasm she would certainly never forget the rest of her life.

Doubt began to creep into her mind. Was it a one off thing? Was it just the desperate impulsiveness of two lonely, sex-starved people?

She was a mature woman. Why couldn't she enjoy the delights of Mohan and not feel guilt? Why couldn't she have sex without involving messy emotions? Right now, it was the last thing she wanted; a relationship doomed to end just as quickly as it started.

The house came into view as they cleared the large gum trees bordering her property.

"My clothes are back there."

He raised a sexy eyebrow and purposefully let his gaze linger on her breast.

"I get clothes later. Pretty, pink, sexy." He wiggled his dark brows playfully, and a big grin broke out over her face.

"You like me naked, huh?"

"Da, very much."

"Well, you have the advantage over me. You've seen everything I have, I want to see everything you have too." She could play the teasing game just as well as he could.

"I no pretty pink like you. I no soft."

"No, you're all man-hard, lovely muscles. And I want to see you." Julia tried pouting as he skipped the two steps of the front porch and strode with her through the opened doors and into her bedroom.

He shook his head with a half grin. "You no like, I have…vat is vord?" He paused. "Scar."

Julia laughed as he set her down on the bed. "Mohan, you do not know me very well at all if you think I would care about scars. Tease me if you want, but you are the sexiest, buffest guy I've ever met. I want to see you naked, scars and all."

He bent over and kissed her forehead. "Later," he murmured against her skin, but Julia was not convinced he would. He deliberately avoided eye contact. He turned and left her in the bedroom, returning a moment later with ice wrapped in a small towel.

"What I need is a hot shower then the ice pack on the ankle. It should be right as rain after that."

"You rest first. I make you food then shower." He folded his arms, and his tone was firm.

"I thought you worked for me," she muttered feeling slightly bullied, but at the same time, cared for.

"I vork. Take care of Julia, or she no pay," he grinned as he said the words.

But still, she could not help feeling a little stung by the implication she was nothing more to him than his paycheck. She crossed her arms over her naked breasts.

"At least could you get me some clothes from one of the boxes so I don't freeze to death" she snapped.

He studied her for a moment before complying with her request. She watched him rummage though her boxes of clothes and grin when he pulled out a black silk teddy. She had never worn it and had forgotten she even packed it.

Julia's mouth gaped as he handed the flimsy material to her. Before she could draw a breath, he speared his hand through her hair and gripped the back of her neck. He held her captive. Controlling the angle of her head, his mouth descended swiftly onto hers. His kiss was deep and passionate, leaving her dazed and breathless when he pulled back.

Seemingly unaffected, Mohan straightened, and with a whistle, strode out of her bedroom. He closed the door behind him, leaving her bewildered, and very turned on.

"Damn you, Mohan!" she yelled only to hear him chuckle. "You'll get yours," she muttered, but she couldn't contain a smile. She liked this cheeky, playful side of Mohan. Wow, what a way to round out an afternoon. Things had taken a surprising turn. The only concern now was where it would lead--and when it would end.

Chapter Ten

Mo had not turned up after dark, and she was worried. She had limped from her spot by the fire to the door, hoping to catch a glimpse of white in the darkness. She sucked in a deep breath and called. "Here Mo! Here, kitty, kitty!"

"Vot you doing?"

Mohan, with a bundle of wood for the fire in his arms, walked around the side of her house. From the light behind her, she could clearly see Mohan's face, and he was very evidently irritated.

"I'm worried about Mo."

He shook his head, climbing the steps to the entranceway of the door. He towered over her, so she hopped back on her good foot to let him in. He walked across the room and put the wood down by the fire.

"He big cat. You no vorry. You..." Brushing his arms of dirt, he turned around and stalked back towards her. "...you no be valking on ankle."

He bent and smoothly scooped his arm under her leg and lifted her off her feet. He shoved the door closed with a swift kick.

"Hey, you don't have to carry me. It feels better at any rate," she lied. Her voice always pitched a little higher when she tried to lie. He raised a dark, disbelieving eyebrow, which set her heart aflutter and made her body begin to heat and melt in his arm. Did the man have any idea how he affected her?

He set her down in the chair by the fire; a packing box he had set up with a pillow on top. As if to prove a point, he gripped her ankle and applied firm pressure over where it was strapped. When she yelped in pain, he let her go. He gave her a smug look of *I told you so.*

She folded her arms and pouted. "Fine, you win that one."

"Stubborn voman. Do as told, stay off ankle."

"Bully," she muttered, but she failed to hide her grin. Mohan turned his back to her as he stoked the fire again.

"Maybe you could go out and look for Mo," she started again.

He gave a huff of obvious annoyance. Placing another log on the fire and jabbing at it with a poker. "No talk of cat. He care for himself."

"He usually turns up after dark. Maybe he doesn't like you, being male and all. I think Mo thinks I'm his girlfriend or something. I read somewhere that male pets become possessive of their owners and get all out of joint when another male is around."

Mohan swiveled around and stared at her in a manner which left her baffled. He sucked in a deep breath, letting it out slowly as if trying to stay calm. He lowered his gaze and shook his head, making his shoulder length hair move from side to side. Julia fought the sudden impulse of wanting to run her fingers through his dark tresses. She swallowed, staring at him. He was focused on other things.

Why was he so opposed to her wanting to find Mo? Something was going on in his head. She was almost afraid to ask.

"You know vhat tiger think?" His question made her sit back and fold her arms across her chest.

"I consider myself a responsible pet owner, so sue me if I care." She was now feeling a bit miffed herself.

He straightened and turned. In two small steps he reached her chair and knelt down beside her.

"You care very much. Have beautiful heart, shows pond reflection of beautiful woman. No more thinking of tiger. I make you forget."

Julia's brows knit together in puzzlement. "That's just silly. How could you make me forget about Mo?"

A secret smile spread across his lips. It made her heart gather speed. Her eyes widened as he reached for her and slid his hands around the back of her neck, drawing her forward.

The heat from his body sent renewed spikes of arousal through her. His warm breath fanned her face as his lips hovered near hers.

Julia trembled, knowing her heart was starting to melt along with her body. If things kept going as they had started, she was going to fall--deeply. Danger signs of getting emotionally involved with Mohan flashed at the back of her brain, but as his lips brushed against hers… Damn, she wanted to take the bull by the horns, no matter the risk.

Julia struggled with herself, fought to stay in control, as he tenderly kissed her lips and his fingers slid through her hair, cradling her head. His lips moved to the corner of her mouth where he placed soft, teasing kisses down along her chin. He tilted her head back to trace his tongue and lips over her neck. She was fighting a losing battle.

"Mohan?" she breathed softly. He pulled back and met her anxious gaze.

She was not sure what was going on behind his eyes. What was she to him? A convenient romp? Was she someone to use in order find his way in the world? He was an illegal immigrant, after all. What happened if they found him and took him from her?

"I see questions in beauty's eyes." His expression held tender concern.

She liked that about Mohan; how easily he seemed to read her. His hand had come to rest on the side of her throat, his fingers feathered over the pulse in her neck.

His intimate, gentle touch was not making her thoughts any clearer. "Ask. Be no frightened."

"I don't know anything about you. How do I know I am safe with you? I've come out of a bad marriage, from a man who hurt me deeply. Sex is one thing, but I need to know what I am to you."

The old Julia would have been too afraid to ask such a thing. She would ponder and stew, not really knowing what was going on.

The lesson she had learned from life and her marriage was she no longer wanted to live in a world of ignorance and constant self-doubt.

Being upfront and honest, firstly with herself then everyone else around her, was the best strategy to prevent misunderstanding. It may not stop her getting hurt, but it would always help her know where she stood.

The air was almost still around him as he stared at her, not giving away any sign of what he was thinking.

"Vat you are is *krasIvaya*, is voman vhich has stolen my breath. You vant promise of future, I no can give. Vot do man hiding have to give?"

Julia thought of several things right off the top of her head.

"Your friendship, your trust, your talents, your skills." *Your heart.* "You shouldn't be hiding, Mohan. I am sure my lawyer could get you asylum. And what is a *krasIvaya?*"

He brushed the hair from her face. "Da. All I am, I give to you. *KrasIvaya* mean my beautiful voman." He leaned back in, brushing his lips over hers. She kissed him back. Then he pulled away, and Julia mourned his woefully brief kiss.

"I ask trust. I no hurt you, please no tell no vone I be here. There is still big danger. No vant my *krasIvaya* in danger."

Julia pondered just how bad a situation he had run from. From the anguish and pain in his expression, it must have been something truly horrifying. Her heart won over any argument her brain had. Julia swallowed and nodded.

"I won't tell anyone. I'm giving you my trust, and I'm going to trust you not to hurt me. I just hope you will one day soon tell me what it is you ran from."

"Da, vone day. Thank you, Julia."

She smiled as he pressed his forehead against hers in silent thanks.

Then she gave him a sudden, impish grin. "Besides, I know what talents you really have."

Mohan wiggled his dark eyebrows playfully. "Da, ve make good sex."

"No, ve make very good sex," Julia giggled, mimicking his accent.

Chapter Eleven

"I hungry," Mohan announced, breaking away from her and rising to his feet.

Julia huffed in annoyance. Men were always thinking about their stomachs. Couldn't he tell he had a very willing and aroused woman ready to rip off his clothes? She nodded towards the new refrigerator humming quietly in the kitchen area.

"Well, go raid the fridge. There's plenty to eat, just don't expect…hey!"

While she had been glancing towards the kitchen, Mohan picked her up into his arms again and carried her through to the bedroom.

"I hungry not for food. Vant to lick and eat you."

"Oh!" Julia's face flamed red as she vividly recalled her tiger having almost done the same thing. He chuckled as he set her down on the bed, holding her gaze.

"Trust me, da?" he asked in all seriousness.

She licked her lips, responding with a "da" of her own.

"Good. I make sex very good for you." The wicked smile of intent doubled her pulse rate in under a split second. She both dreaded and craved what he was going to do.

He left her and moved around the bed to the three boxes of clothes she'd brought with her. She watched as he flipped open one of them and began sifting through the contents, pulling out several of her satin and silk scarves.

At the mere thought of what he was going to do with them, Julia's lower stomach clenched and juices flooded her between her thighs. She never had the opportunity to be sexually adventurous. Try as she might to please Richard, he took no interest in anything other than straight missionary style sex with her and maybe the odd blowjob.

Mohan stalked towards her with clear intent in his crystal clear, icy gaze. He set down the scarves by her hip. Her breath hitched as he swiftly climbed on the bed, his large frame hovering over her. When she tilted her head back to meet his gaze, he swooped down, and captured her mouth with his.

Unlike the little light nibbles he had delivered earlier, his mouth was hard, hot, and his tongue pushed passed her lips. He demanded and took what he wanted from her, stealing the breath from her lungs.

Hot hands parted her jumper and shirt from her pants, making her shiver with both his touch and the cool of the air. Brief disappointment filled her as he broke the kiss to tug the clothing over her head. Air whooshed as they were tossed aside. Then he was back devouring her mouth. She never even noticed her bra vanish until his hand cupped her breast, molding the plump flesh into his palm.

His other hand skimmed across her stomach and to her side. The pursuit of pleasure at Mohan's hands, mouth, and body dominated her thoughts. His hand left her breast, mirroring his other as he touched and caressed her hips.

"So soft, *krasIvaya.*" He broke the kiss, drawing breath against her lips. He took hold of her wrists in a gentle but firm grasp and drew them across her body and above her head. She felt the silk of a scarf wrap around her skin, replacing the heat of his hands. He had tied her to the bed head.

~ * ~

There were questions in her dark blue depths, but he was relieved to see no fear when he secured her wrists--but not too tightly. Her trust made his heart pound, and a feeling of possessive pride filled him. He wanted to keep her trust, yet he also knew his secret could be the one thing that could tear the fragile bond between them. Just like the fragile material securing her wrists, if she pulled hard enough, it would rend the fabric and free her.

He skimmed his hands down her arms. She had such soft skin and touching her was a simple pleasure in itself. She squirmed and giggled tugging against her bonds.

Mohan realized she was ticklish, and a devilish grin spread across his face. The sound of Julia's laughter was sweet music to his ears.

He wanted to feel her skin pressed against his. He wanted to show her a world of pleasure she seemed naive of. He knew he could not let her see him, or what lay beneath the precious clothing she had selflessly given him.

Tying her was firstly to stop her touching, but the second scarf was going to prevent her from seeing. It was such a stunning sight, her helpless and naked before him. His gaze was riveted to her breasts as her chest moved with each breath she took. Her lovely wide eyes staring up at him with absolute trust both tore at his heart and made him ache to the point of pain. He wanted to sink himself inside of her and imprint himself on her soul for eternity.

He scooped up her black and white satin scarf and placed it over her eyes, careful not to snag her hair as he tied it. Her breathing automatically quickened as her other senses kicked into a heightened gear.

He could feel the trembling of her body, but he was far from finished with his naked beauty. He was going to finish what he had started in the yard when she was bathing. He was going to lick and nibble on her core until she screamed; lap up all the intimate musky flavours that drove him wild and made him purr loudly. Only then would he sheath himself deeply into her and take his pleasure.

Satisfied the blindfold was secure, Mohan moved off the bed and stripped his clothes. He settled himself back on the bed beside her, determined to explore every inch of her body with his.

~ * ~

Anticipation was a killer. She tugged on her restraints--not hard enough to break them, although Julia knew she could if she really tried. But the thrill of not knowing what he was going to do to her was making her skin prickle.

The first touch of his hot mouth against her breast made her gasp as the wet flick of his tongue danced over her nipple. When he blew cool air across it, it tightened. It was a strange, almost…pain, but also an extremely pleasurable sensation. With each lap of his tongue, the feeling speared through her body, centering to the core of her sex. Her clit pulsed, feeling engorged with blood.

She was instantly reminded of the way Mo had tasted her. Damn, why couldn't she push that damn cat out of her mind! It was a human man pleasuring her to insanity, not a damn tiger!

A moan tore from low in her throat as he covered the breast with his lips, sucking it deep into the cavern of his mouth. His hand caressed her lower stomach, and his thick fingers threaded through the curls at the junction of her thighs.

She arched into his hand as his fingers parted her wet folds and found her sensitive nub. The dual sensation of him flicking a finger across her clit and sucking on her nipple had her crying out. She writhed and panted, as he pushed her toward release. But before she could come, he pulled back his hand and let go of her right breast.

"Oh god, Mohan! Don't stop, damn it." Frustration laced in her tone.

"Good sex for vating voman." Amusement was threaded through his tone.

Damn it, it wasn't funny. She wanted to come.

He silenced her protest with his lips, spearing his tongue deeply into her mouth and pulling back to nibble on her lower lip. Then he jumped his kisses down to her left breast and began the touching all over again, bringing her to the peak before pulling back.

She felt him move away from her, leaving her panting and writhing on the bed. His hands gripped her under her knees and pushed them up against her stomach. She was wide open; exposed and very vulnerable.

She felt his hot breath on her open sex right before the molten heat of his tongue touched her clit. Good god, she forgot to breathe as the pure fire spread through her. Already at the peak, her body suddenly stilled in a tight spasm with the long swipe of his tongue; she burst apart from the inside out.

Where she got the breath to scream, she had no idea, but the room filled with her high pitched keen as her body was thrown over the edge of the universe and into pure bliss, quaking with the most incredible orgasms she'd ever known.

Strangely, she could have sworn Mohan was purring. Her pleasure-drunken brain could not be sure. Mohan had no mercy on her trembling body. He speared his tongue deep into her core, lapping up the juices that flowed from her body as he tongue fucked her. Pushing her into a new frenzy, she needed to feel him penetrate her, feel his hard length deep within her.

The heat of his mouth left her, and she felt him lift her hips, keeping her legs folded and pinned against her chest, the head of his cock connected with her willing, weeping sex. He groaned as he slid in inch by agonizing inch, slowly filling her until he could go no further.

He uttered words in Russian. The way the words rolled of his tongue heightened the pleasure of their intimate connection.

Withdrawing almost all the way, he thrust back deeply, making her gasp in delight at the delicious friction.

Unable to touch him, her hands gripped the curled iron of the bed frame as he powered home, time and time again, clearly seeking his own pleasure. From the angle of his penetration, Julia knew he hit the mythical pleasure spot within her body, driving her body towards another explosive release.

"Julia, Julia, Julia," he uttered her name like a reverent prayer.

Unable to hold back the sensation, she threw back her head and screamed her release. Mohan gave a snarl, and she felt his body shake and his cock pulse within her as he came.

She was still quaking with her own release as Mohan stilled, deeply imbedded inside her.

A sudden whoosh of air that sounded like a gunshot ripped through the room. Julia screamed with sudden terror of the unknown. Mohan growled menacingly, much like her tiger would, and leapt off her. She heard the grunts and yells of two men. She tugged hard against her restraints, and the silk tore under her frantic yanking. She twisted around to rip off her blindfold, blinking rapidly against the lamplight from the corner.

What she saw confused her. Mohan had a struggling man pinned securely to the floor.

"Mrs Cooper!" the trapped man managed to squeal out as Mohan pressed a rather impressive naked knee into the center of his back, squeezing his lungs.

It took a moment for her to realize it was John Leeman from the real estate agency. What struck her senseless was the fact Mohan had the most amazing body tattoo she had ever seen in her life. Was this what he hadn't wanted her to see? Tattooed stripes, almost identical to the stripes of her white tiger, spread from the top of his shoulders, down and across his simply fine, firm ass, and down his legs.

Beautiful muscles bulged as they strained to keep Mr Leeman pinned. Mohan turned his head, and she met his angry, icy stare. It snapped her out of her obvious gawking.

"Will you tell your beast to get the hell off me!" Mr Leeman demanded, the fear and pain evident in his voice.

Mohan growled louder at his words.

Julia scrambled off the bed. She bit into her lip to stop the sudden cry of pain as she had forgotten about her ankle. Balancing on one foot, she snatched her robe, which was hanging over the end of the bed railing and quickly tugged it on.

"Mohan, that is John Leeman, the real estate agent from Bonang. You had better let him go."

She couldn't keep her eyes off his rippling, lean muscled body. It was amazing, beautiful. Why would Mohan be ashamed of such a thing? She wondered if it was some Siberian tribal thing they did. Did Siberia even have tribes? Her mind bubbled with so many questions.

"Damn it, get the hell off me! I'm gonna call the cops!"

Mr Leeman's words sent a jolt of anger and fear through her. Careful not to put too much pressure on her ankle, she leaned down and saw his portly face reddened in anger and embarrassment.

"Before he lets you go, just what are you doing here?"

"It's not against the law to pay a damn social call," he hissed.

"Vant me to kill him?" Mohan asked her coolly.

She stared at him. Surely he was kidding.

"Um, no. I think what we have here is a misunderstanding. Please, Mohan, let him go," she pleaded softly.

Mohan gave a grunt and released his tight grip. He pulled back his knee and gracefully rose to his feet.

Anger still blazed in Mohan's eyes. She didn't know to whom it was directed. At her? At Leeman? Hell, she was very angry with Leeman for bursting in on them.

Breaking eye contact, he moved and walked out the open door, Mohan paused as Leeman rose to his feet.

"Lay vone finger on her, I vill kill you," he warmed Leeman before stalking out.

Breaking eye contact, he moved and walked out the open door as Leeman rose to his feet. A moment later she heard the sound of water running in her new shower.

"Misunderstanding, indeed. Had I known you were being screwed stupid and not being attacked, I wouldn't have burst in," Leeman glowered indignantly as he climbed to his feet. "Who the hell is he?"

"Who he is, is none of your business. I am a single woman and can entertain who I want, how I want." She folded her arms defensively across her breasts. She was sure Leeman had copped a good eyeful of her naked and tied to the bed.

Leeman's face was still red as he leered at her. "Yes, I see that. Playing sex bondage games with a tattooed freak. If I had known you swung that way, I would have been happy to accommodate you."

Anger curled deep into her belly. Any thought of being nice to John Leeman evaporated with his nasty remark.

"You are a rude and obtrusive man. Get the hell out of my house and off my property before I call the police on you for trespassing."

She was not sure his face could get any redder than it was, but clearly she was wrong.

"You don't know who you're dealing with," he warned.

"I think you've made yourself very clear. I know exactly who I am dealing with. Get out, now!"

Leeman swiveled on his heel and stomped back through the house. Then Julia hobbled down the hall to shut the door Leeman had left open.

"I'm gonna need to buy a new lock and a bolt," she muttered to herself, taking several deep breaths and trying to bring some calm to her shaking hands.

Hearing that the water had stopped running, Julia made her way to the bathroom as quickly as she was able.

Mohan and his amazing tattoo was foremost in her thoughts. She had questions, the biggest one being, why the heck would he want to hide his tattoo from her?

A cloud of steam met her as she pushed open the bathroom door. "Mohan, the rude man has gone."

One towel was wrapped around his lean waist, another he used to rub dry his hair, which was all damp and disheveled. She didn't think it was possible, but he was even sexier like this. From the hard line of his mouth and angry expression, something was bothering him.

"I go too." He made to move past her.

"Why?" She stood in his way, refusing to let him pass. "Don't let that idiot chase you off. You don't need to go anywhere."

He met her gaze. "You see vhat freak I am, vith markings. You no vant me. I go."

Gee, and she thought women suffered with image complexes! She just grinned at him.

"Freak? Is that what you assume I think of these?" She gestured to his chest, where the stripes came around his side and were not entirely black. They were almost a dark chocolate brown. The thick, mismatched pattern of stripes wrapped almost lovingly around the sides of his body and over his arms and legs. The ones over his chest did not meet in the center. "They're unusual, yes. I've never seen anything like it, but I think it's damn sexy. I never thought I liked tattoos on people until I saw yours."

He appeared stunned, almost disbelieving her words.

"Julia, these no tattoos. I vas borne vith marking. I say I have scar."

He seemed to be waiting for her to make some kind of detrimental remark, to confirm the fact she thought him a freak. She was surprised but not put off in anyway.

"Whole people in my village born different. Vhat is vhy they come, they kill…" he faltered.

Julia suddenly had a good inkling of why he was running, why he was hiding. The anguish in Mohan's beautiful eyes broke her heart.

"You are not a freak, and you're no different from me or any other person. You have red blood running though your veins, a heart that beats. I don't care what you were born with, Mohan. You're still a man and someone I…" Julia hesitated. "…someone I care for very much. And you're still sexy as hell. I don't care if you believe me or not, it's the truth. No one and nothing can change that."

She moved in closer, placing her hand on his warm chest and delighting in the feel of his hot skin. "All I am asking of you is to have a little faith in me. I am not the kind of person to betray you or think poorly of you just because of this." She feathered her fingers across one of the patterns. "Did I mention how sexy you are? Trust me in this. You are the most beautiful man I've ever met and even more so without clothes on."

The flash of emotion on Mohan's face was hard to describe. She wanted to comfort him and see the smile that made her heart pound; to gain his full trust. Yet, she knew he was still hiding something deeper.

He held her gaze. Then he drew in a breath before speaking. "I believe you."

She could see he was struggling to hide the emotion in his voice. He took her hands into his, turning them over to kiss her palms. "I be back in morning. I go now."

She didn't want him to leave, but she also understood he needed his space and time to think, not some clingy woman smothering him. Releasing her hand, he stepped back.

Julia gave him a warm smile. "Okay. Thank you for tonight, the rude man aside. You can tie me to the bed anytime."

Her comment was enough to make his lips twitch up at the corners. His small smile was enough reassurance for now. She hobbled back to let him pass, closing the bathroom door behind him. She leaned against it and drew in a breath before releasing it in a soft sigh.

It seemed her life problems were small and petty compared to the suffering Mohan must have gone through.

She wanted to help him, no matter the cost to herself.

"Damn it, girl. You should have learnt your lesson," she muttered to herself as she limped across to the bathtub. She twisted the shower knobs and the water flowed down, steaming hot. She stripped off her clothes and climbed in. With a resigned sigh, she knew it was useless and she was helpless. Just as easily as the water cascaded down over her skin, she knew she had fallen in love.

Chapter Twelve

Leeman still simmered over his untimed entry into Julia Cooper's house. The vision of her tied to the bed with a freaky, albeit handsome, younger man fucking her refused to leave his head. His pride was wounded when the tattooed beast had attacked him and, still naked, pinned him to the floor.

In hindsight, he supposed he could have been more diplomatic about the situation, but he was too angry and turned on in the same instance to care about being polite. Any plans of wooing the not so lonely woman had been thrown out the window.

There was always another way. A sinister smile curled his lips as he pulled into the driveway of his house. Slamming the car door, he stalked up the gravel path to his empty, cold home.

Once inside, he headed directly to his office. Starting the heater, he sat down behind his computer. His thoughts turned to the man Julia was fucking. Other than appearing much younger than the divorced woman, from the accent apparent in the few words he had spoken, it was clear he was Russian. And what was with the tiger-stripe tattoos? Was he some kind of act that had escaped from the Moscow Circus?

Leeman pondered this as his computer booted and connected to the Internet. She had called him Mohan. Apart from that, he had no other details, but a man like that would stand out. He was too different to ignore. Someone, somewhere would know about him.

Leeman started tapping away on his keyboard. He was good with computers, but most of all, he had a talent for finding out things other people wanted to hide.

If Julia was hiding this freak from immigration or something similar, he would soon know. Then he would make them pay.

~ * ~

Mohan had not slept well. He had stayed away from the house--and the woman within. He and his tiger pined to be by her side, surrounded by the comfort and warmth of her body. He had rested in the hollow of a large burnt out gum tree in his tiger form. He had left his clothes neatly folded in the old farm work shed.

The cold of the night air, along with the tumult in his mind, had kept him awake, thinking about the woman, his past and how he could make things better for her and himself.

Her open acceptance of him had drained his anger about being exposed. Her open honesty of just how she saw him soothed his fear of her rejection. She had been kind hearted, yet fierce, in the way she had defended him.

The need for Julia had now surpassed an outward need of clothing and food. It was a deeper longing for the comfort of a woman and a home to call his. He could not change the past. He needed to move on with his life, and here he had just what he needed: a territory to claim and cubs to raise.

What she did not realize was now, after they had coupled, after he had come inside her, there was no possibility of him leaving, even if she did reject him. Pure mating instinct had overruled the thought of protecting Julia from his seed--he wanted it inside her, making her his. Even though he did not know of any woman to have become pregnant to his kind, he was well aware of the fact she could be carrying his cubs. The thought brought a low growl to his throat. If she was not carrying his cubs, he would soon make sure she was.

It put a whole new perspective on his relationship with the woman. He still did not know what her reaction was going to be when he finally did reveal what he was.

Just like all the other chances he had taken thus far with Julia, it was another risk he was now willing to take. She had more than proven her worth. She was beautiful, not just in body, but of heart and soul. She was a most valuable prize worth claiming.

Here and now with Julia was the start of a new future.

As the dawn broke, he rose and crawled from his hiding place, shaking the dew from his fur. The nocturnal creatures had settled for the day, and this creature had a woman to claim. She had already confessed to loving his tiger half; how hard would it be for her to love him as a man? He wanted it, craved it.

He knew she had become aroused when he had licked her with his tiger tongue, how divine her skin tasted. He began to ponder just how far he could push her boundaries before revealing he was both man and tiger.

He would soon find out.

Another issue, which he worried about, was Julia's wealth. It was not in his nature to constantly take what he had not earned and was not his. He needed to find a way to support himself--and her.

Once he became more settled, he would find a job other than mending their home.

Home--the thought warmed him. He wanted to give her something other than just his body and his skills as her lover. He stretched his forepaws and sharpened his claws on a nearby tree. As his claws shredded the bark, an idea came to him. A claiming gift would not go astray and would help her accept him even more.

Mohan trotted back to the house. She had left out a pile of meat for Mo. He smiled inwardly at her selfless generosity towards his tiger. He gratefully ate his meal, the meat still fresh in the cold night air. He went back to the shed and shifted. Then, dressed once again, he grabbed a chain and a saw and headed back into the thick of the forest trees.

~ * ~

At least she knew Mo had been around: the large stainless steel plate she had left him the night before had been licked clean of the meat she had piled on it.

It had been a fitful night's sleep without either Mohan or Mo by her side. Mohan was in the shed, hammering and sawing away. She did not dare go out to him, still wanting to give him plenty of space.

At least her ankle was feeling better. She made herself a cup of tea and contemplated what to do next. Thanks to Mohan's vigilant work, her bathroom was completed. The spare room was also near completion, but it still needed a few homey touches. The meal area held her camp table and two chairs. She needed a table and chairs, a sofa, rugs, curtains. Sighing, she sat down and wrote a list.

With notepad in hand, she made her way out to the shed to ask Mohan if there was anything he wanted or needed.

Her heart stammered in her chest as he came into view. She paused at the open door of the shed and watched. His shirtsleeves were rolled up, and she could see the lines where his marks ended. The beautiful display of muscles bunched and flexed as he guided the block of sandpaper over the timber. The view held her enthralled.

He was sanding down what must have been a tree he had felled in the forest. As if sensing her there, he straightened before turning around just in time to catch her staring at him.

She could not help the rise of heat which crept into her cheeks. She blinked and swallowed, trying to regain the part of her brain, which had stopped thinking the moment she saw him.

"Good morning," she greeted, keeping her smile welcoming and friendly. He gave her a nod. His gaze roamed lazily down her body then up again, sending a spike of heat through her.

"Ankle good, da?"

"Yes, thank you. It feels fine today. How are you this morning?"

"Cold, vithout voman by side. Did much thinking of your vords."

Although surprised by his words, they were not unwelcome. He was being open to confess such a thing to her.

"I didn't sleep much either," she said trying to hide the uncertainty of her new feeling towards Mohan.

She waited as he paused to think of the right English words. He set aside his safety glasses and brushed the sawdust from his clothes. Julia's mouth went dry seeing his hungry expression as he strode towards her.

She had to tilt her head to keep his gaze, feeling a thrill as he reached for her hand and drew her into his arms. He dipped his head to brush his lips over hers. Her arms slid up to his shoulders and her fingers curled into his shirt as he increased the pressure, kissing her thoroughly, passionately. The world around her vanished, and there was nothing but the man holding her, kissing her.

He pulled back, leaving her dazed and breathless. She gazed up at him in awe and wonder.

"You very special voman--my voman. I vant to keep close. I vant to trust. No vant to lose."

Her heart skipped a beat at his words: *his woman.* She very much liked the sound of that. Maybe, just maybe, she could let her heart have hope of a future with Mohan.

She ran her tongue along her bottom lip. The exotic masculine flavour of him lingered. "You won't lose me, Mohan. For as long as you want, I am yours."

Approval of her words shone proud in his eyes. "I no like other man. Vill not hurt my Julia."

"Good." She interlocked her fingers around the back of his neck. "Because I am liable to scratch out the eyes of any woman who looks at you. I want my scrummy Siberian man all to myself."

He chuckled and wicked carnal thoughts started running through her head. "You know what I want to do tonight?"

She loved the way his eyebrow would arch in curiosity. She was starting to identify his moods and frames of mind just from his expressive face.

"Vat do you vant to do?"

Julia could also see he was using her words, repeating certain phrases back to her to help improve his English. He was a smart man.

On tippy toes she pulled him down to whisper in his ear. "I want to find every single stripe you have and trace them with my tongue." She nipped at his earlobe, feeling quite the sexy vixen as she pulled away with a wicked grin on her face.

His eyes darkened with a thunderstorm of desire, making her feel like she was sitting in a dinky little boat, in the middle of the sea, and Mohan was the oncoming storm--thrilling yet terrifying, and way out of her depth.

She was going to hold onto all that was Mohan: his vulnerabilities, his amazing strength, even his dark and dangerous secrets.

Was this what it was like, she wondered, to truly fall in love?

Richard had never evoked such turbulent emotions within her. All she ever had with him was worry and pain. She had believed herself to be in love with him when they had married. But after the ring was on her finger, Richard had always remained distant. She was a stepping-stone to him in the company; marry the boss's daughter and climb the corporate ladder to success.

Mohan's grip on her tightened as he pulled her into the old shed and pushed her up against the workbench. She could feel the hard bulge in his pants pressing into her hip.

"My vicked voman." His amused tone was husky and rough with desire, sending an erotic shiver down her spine.

She thought about her words. "Yes, you make me think wicked thoughts and want to do reckless things. I don't understand it, but I don't feel restrained or timid around you."

"Feel freedom, da?"

"You're right. You make me feel free." She knew it was not just sexual freedom, losing her inhibitions. She was always learning about herself. Knowing the fact she never really loved Richard had suddenly eased a huge weight from her shoulders, and it had given her the freedom to love Mohan as she did.

His fingers brushed her hair from her shoulders, and his lips started to nip and suck at her flesh.

"Vhy vate for tonight? I vant my voman now." His hand skimmed from her waist and under her jacket. She jolted. Her breathing became rapid as he touched her skin and cupped her breast through the fabric of her bra.

"Because… " She struggled to hold in a moan as he squeezed. The feeling of his lips made her want to give in, to have him fuck her right here on the bench.

"…I need to go into town."

"Vhy?" He nibbled his way up and over her chin. His nimble fingers had already unhooked the top button of her jeans, and he eased down the zipper. His lips reached the corner of her mouth. She was having trouble thinking. Why was it, again, she needed to go to town? She was trembling with desire.

Before she could answer, he covered her mouth with his, his tongue pushing past her lips sliding deeply into her mouth in a dominating kiss. One strong arm wrapped around her waist as he lifted her clear off the ground.

The cold wood of the bench on her ass did nothing to dampen the fire of her passion, nor did the cool air on her heated skin, as he moved slightly back to remove her top. Damn, the man had quick skills when it came to getting her naked!

Any plans and thoughts of what she wanted to do flew out the shed door as her legs automatically wrapped around his waist. She had no idea what to think and didn't care as his plundering mouth left her dizzy. She whimpered when he pulled back slightly and pulled her legs away from his waist. He pulled off her jeans, casting them carelessly aside. In the next moment he was back on her, kissing her feverously. She kissed him back just as hungrily, needing him with a lust which surpassed her sense of reason.

When he pulled back, they both were panting, with need. His gaze hungrily raked down her exposed body, the burning passion in his pale depths, making her feel like a wanton sex goddess.

Perched on one hand, she managed to wedge her other hand between them before he could tug her back into his arms.

His raised an eyebrow. She knew he questioned why she had done it.

"Take yours off too," she managed to order huskily. She would be damned if she would let him get away with not fully undressing this time. He hesitated, a moment of uncertainty flashing through his expression, then he reached for the hem of his shirt and tugged it up and over his head, laying it carefully over the other side of the workbench then his jeans were on the floor.

Julia licked her lips, wanting to purr at the sight of all the beautifully striped flesh and muscle exposed for her viewing pleasure. She beckoned with her hand, and as he moved in she met his gaze, showing him how sincere she was about wanting to touch him. She was trying, without words, to show him how beautiful she found him to be.

She explored with her hands, delighting in his heated skin, and the feel of his hard muscles beneath the smooth flesh. She loved the way it flexed as she skimmed her hand lower over his set of fine abs.

"You remind me of Mo," she said without thinking. "Big, strong, and the most amazing thing I've ever beheld."

There it was again; his expression was one she could not quite decipher. Was he pleased or angry she had compared him to the tiger? He caught her hand and held it against his firm flesh.

"I am tiger, and he is me. Ve are vone," he said and tensed as he awaited her reaction.

Well, he had stripes like Mo, but he was a man. She didn't know what kind of genetic makeup had given him the birthmarks, but it didn't matter. He referred to himself as a tiger, which was understandable. Also, considering how he and Mo were much the same, they were both powerful creatures from Siberia, she could only guess the tiger was a symbol or totem in his village.

She simply gave him a sinful smile. "I can see that, and I don't care. I just want to make you purr, big boy," she teased.

With a low growl Mohan gripped her upper arms, pulling her flush against his beautiful hard length. Her head tipped back to meet his lips with hers, kissing him back feverishly. Her hands reached to touch every part of him she could.

Her bra slid from between them, meshing her breasts against his chest. Her legs wrapped around his waist again.

She wanted to crawl under his skin, have him embedded so deeply within her that she wouldn't know where he started or she ended.

He slid one arm around her back, making her arch toward him. He broke the kiss and lowered his head to attach his mouth to her aching nipple.

She let out a long moan of pleasure as his mouth encased her flesh, his tongue twirling around her hardened bud. He nipped at it with his teeth, sending jolts straight down to her clit.

Oh god, she never wanted it to stop. His free hand cupped the other breast, squeezing in time with his suckling. He switched sides to worship the other with equal attention.

Her fingers threaded through his soft, dark hair, cradling his head as he laved. She moaned. He softly growled.

Feeling her body could not take any more; she reached a point of pure desperation. "Oh, Mohan. I need you." She tugged on his hair gently.

He responded by capturing her wrists in his strong hands and pinning them by her sides. The action of being restrained made her hotter and wetter. He pushed her backwards onto the bench.

"Not finished tasting." His deep response rumbled against her skin. She shifted her legs over his shoulder. Julia knew what was coming: the man had a tongue just as wicked as Mo's. She wanted it, she craved it.

At the first touch of his tongue on her slit, her breath hitched. Her body tensed for a split second before she let out a long moan and relaxed into the wet heat of his raspy tongue. Strangely, it felt different this time, raspier just like Mo.

He gave a long lick before sucking her swollen nub into his mouth, tugging with successive, strong pulls. They sent her reeling with overloaded sensations, her keening cry filling the air as every nerve ending exploded in pure ecstasy.

Mohan pulled away from her. She cried out in protest, and he swiftly lifted her from the bench and spun her around. He pushed her down onto her hands and knees on the dirt floor.

Her body still trembled as his large hands squeezed into the flesh of her hips. He clasped her tightly and shoved her legs wide with his own. She felt the head of his cock prodding between her ass cheeks. It slid down and connected with the mouth of her sex.

She was stretched wide as Mohan mounted her fully and deeply. His hot cock pulled back before swiftly burrowing again into her wet channel, over and over with the force of a hammer blow. She was rocked forward on the ground. She grunted in animal lust as he reignited the heat within her belly. He was deep inside, driving her towards another violent climax.

Mohan fell forward on her, his arm wound so tightly around her waist she had trouble breathing. His hand slipped between the fold of her sex and found her hyper sensitive clit. He pinched it, and that motion pitched her over the edge. She screamed loud and long.

Mohan snarled, his body shaking as he pushed to the hilt. He stilled, clasping her closely against his chest. She felt his cock pulsing along the walls of her inner channel as he came, panting breathlessly in her ear. She did not know how long they stayed locked together. Slowly, she began breathing again and regained some level of normality, softly moaning as he slid from her. He trailed little kisses over her shoulder and down her spine as he moved off her.

She yelped and turned her head to glare at him when he nipped her ass cheek. She was greeted by a mischievous grin.

She giggled as he rose gracefully to his feet and offered his hand. She placed her hand into his, and he pulled her up, watching as she brushed the dark dirt from her knees and the palms of her hands.

"I've heard of dirty sex, but I didn't think they meant it literally."

He chuckled, pulling her into his arms then wrapped them tightly around her.

"Dirty sex good, da? We now go have clean sex in shower."

Julia laughed, gazing up into his pale blue depths and felt light hearted and salacious.

She pulled from his arms, very aware he watched her every move. She gathered her strewn clothes and, still very naked, walked out of the shed.

"Well," she called over her shoulder, wiggling her ass at him, "shower's this way."

How Mohan moved so fast, she had no idea, but she gave a delighted squeal when she found herself scooped up in his strong arms. He barreled them both back towards the house.

Chapter Thirteen

At thirty-five, Julia had just discovered what she had been missing from her life. She stretched lazily, wincing at the sore twinges between her thighs. She glanced down her naked body, and a salacious smile curved her lips at the little love tokens Mohan had left all over her pale skin.

It was not just great sex--it was a newfound confidence that came with finding your own sense of self worth.

Caring what others thought about what she said or did had held her back from truly experiencing life. No longer. She was not going to be the doormat everyone had always expected her to be.

She had taken the first step with the divorce. Mind you, her pit bull of a lawyer had also helped her win that victory.

She tossed aside the covers and rolled from the bed. With swing in her hips, she strode through the house towards the bathroom like a well-satisfied goddess.

It was getting late. Mohan had kissed the curve of her back before returning to the shed to finish whatever project he was working on. She still needed to head into town and wanted to make the trip as brief as possible.

Here, she felt at home. It was a comfort she had no desire to be away from for any length of time.

Showered and dressed, she jogged down the porch steps, giving Mohan a wave and a smile as he appeared through the doorway of the shed. His pale blue eyes gleamed. And a knowing smile appeared on his handsome face as she slipped behind the seat of her Rover.

She carefully navigated the long narrow dirt track heading off her property. The thought of Mohan returning to his "place of lodging" did not sit well with her. She had not seen anyplace nearby where he could possibly be staying.

If they were going to establish a relationship, then they certainly needed to have a talk about that. Heck, they needed to talk about quite a few other things as well.

Like the dark cloud she could see looming on the horizon, she feared the secrets he harbored--and the fact he had jumped ship and was living under the radar--would become a stinging backlash of problems.

Large drops splattered on the windscreen. Julia switched on her wipers, and it didn't take long for everything around her to become soaked through.

By the time she got home, they would know how well the roof had been mended.

~ * ~

He'd had seen her expensive Rover pass his office, no doubt to buy more things for her freakish, striped boy toy.

It was raining hard, but it would not impede him from his purpose. Julia Cooper was a means to end his long running debt, and her wealth would set himself up for a good future. He flipped over the *Open* sign on his office door so it said *Closed,* and he stepped through and locked it behind him.

Through the driving rain, he could see she had gone into the town's hardware store. He quickened his step, conscious of the fact his comb-over was being washed away. He ran the rest of the way, shoving the store door open in his haste to get out of the rain. Bent over at the waist, he sucked in several long, deep breaths. He was unaccustomed to running.

Julia was smiling at Matt while the young man studied a little piece of white paper. Leeman quickly ducked out of view behind a tall line of shelving and waited.

Matt headed down to the back of the store. As Julia headed in the same direction, her gaze roamed over the contents of the shelves.

"Hello, Mrs Cooper."

She gasped, startled by John's sudden appearance. Her eyes narrowed, and her lips pursed together in a mixture of distaste and distrust.

"I have nothing to say to you." She moved to step around him.

John quickly grabbed her arm, halting any escape.

"Unhand me right now, Mr Leeman," she hissed in irritation glaring at the spot where he gripped her upper arm.

He did let her go but stood in her path. "We need to have a talk."

Her snort was far from ladylike. "I don't think so."

"Oh, you don't have to do any talking. Just listen, unless you don't really care about the illegal alien you're fucking."

Instantly, she stiffened and folded her arms defensively across her chest.

"That is none of your damn business."

"Oh, but I've made it my business, and I am sure the wonderful people in the immigration office would love to make it their business as well."

From the way she visibly paled, he knew he was on a winning streak. *Gotcha!* he thought in silent triumph. Right away, he knew her Russian freak *was* of value.

"What is it you want?" Her voice was tight with anger.

"You want to keep your little secret, and I want out of this god forsaken dump of a town. So, for me to keep my mouth shut, you're going to pay."

"You're a real estate agent. Don't you make your own damn money?" she responded coolly.

"Not nearly enough for the lifestyle I want. I have habits which need to be funded."

She visibly swallowed. "How much do you want, and what guarantee do I have you will leave us alone if I pay you?"

"I want fifty thousand. Once I have it, I am going to leave town, and you will never hear from me again. You and your freak can live happily ever after." He didn't want to make the sum too much, or she would decide her love was not worth the price.

Her skeptical expression told him she did not believe him. He could care less what she believed--as long as he got what he wanted.

"You want cash? That kind of money would take some arranging. I have a checkbook, but I've left it at the house."

"I know a cheque from you would clear. Bring it to my office in the morning."

She met his gaze and nodded.

"Mrs Cooper?" Matt, the store attendant, called as he appeared around the corner holding a long plank of timber. The young man glanced curiously between them.

John knew it was time to take his leave. He plastered on the same fake smile he used for all his real estate clients.

"Have a good afternoon, Mrs Cooper. I'll see you bright and early in the morning. Then we can discuss our new business arrangement."

She gave a stiff nod before turning her attention to Matt. John spun on his heel and made a beeline for the door; confident he had Mrs Cooper just where he wanted her.

"We're out of cedar, but we do have a large stock load of pine," he heard Matt say.

~ * ~

By the time she arrived at the house, her fingers ached from gripping the steering wheel so tight. Her body was tense with anxiety.

It was near dark. She saw smoke rising from the stone chimney and a light flickering in the window. Mohan must still be home.

Her stomach churned at the thought of losing him. She was caught between a rock and a hard place. Her mind was full of doubt. She hardly knew Mohan, so how could she love him? Was it really love, or just lust? The attraction between them was clearly powerful, but would it last? Maybe she should just pay Mohan the fifty thousand dollars and ask him to leave.

It had stopped raining. The ground was muddy as she slipped from her Rover and slammed the door behind her. She marched up the newly mended steps.

Even before she reached the door, it swung inwards. Mohan's smiling face fell when he saw her obviously distressed state.

His brows knitted together in a scowl as he studied her. She stared back at him, unsure of what to tell him, what to ask him.

"Mohan… "

He took hold of her arm, drawing her into the house and closing the door. He guided her to a chair by the fire.

"Sit. Tell me vhat has happened." His tone was calm and commanding.

"I don't know who you are, and someone has found out you're not living here in Australia legally."

Julia drew in a deep breath in order to stay calm. "The man from the other day, John Leeman, he…he said if I don't pay him money, he's going to expose you to the authorities."

She glanced away. She could not meet his intense gaze and instead focused on the flickering flames of the fire.

"Vat you say?" She could hear the tension in his voice.

Julia tore her gaze from the fire and rose from the chair to face him. "I don't know who you really are. I only get glimpses of what you may have been through. You said you wouldn't hurt me, and I've given you my trust despite what it is you won't tell me. I told Leeman I would pay him the money. Maybe I'm just a crazy, lonely woman, but I will do whatever it takes to protect you."

He raised his hand, gently brushing back several strands of her hair which had fallen across her face. She was unsure of his expression. Was it regret? Disappointment?

"I see you no understand vhen I tell you I be tiger."

She was confused as to why he would refer to that now. His stripes did not matter. She had already established that.

He drew in a deep breath. "My village, ve are all peaceful. Ve no hurt anyvone. Ve vhere born different from others, so people fear us. Ve hide deep in mountain forest, avay from people." Anger darkened his face as he spoke. "Men come vith guns and cages. They kill all my family and friends. I fight, but I get knocked out. Vhen I voke up, I found they had put me in cage like animal. I vas their prisoner. Take me avay from my lands. Vhen I vas on ship, I fight and get free. I run avay, jump into vater.

Vas fate the ship vas passing Australia. Have much pain in heart, much sadness, but meet beautiful voman. She start to heal my vound, help me see I need to have life. I no tell you this, I no vant pity, I no vant my voman in danger from those who kill my people."

The utter, raw pain in his eyes made her heart break instantly, clearing any doubt from her mind. She did love him.

"I am sorry for your losses, for what you have suffered. My heart aches for you."

She stepped in close and wrapped her arms around his waist, laying her head on his chest. She could hear the rhythm of his strong, beating heart beneath her ear. She knew her words were inadequate in that moment, but it was all she had. What does one do or say when confronted with the horrors he had lived through?

She was glad he could take some comfort in her; that she could help him move on with his life.

Her mind raced to think of what she could do. How could she make things better for both of them--and keep leaches like Leeman away from the door?

His arms moved around her, pulling her tighter against his hard length.

"I no care for vhat happen to me. I vant to protect you. I vill kill dis Leeman for making you vorry." There was no mistaking the deadly intent in his tone.

Julia's head jerked back. She stared up at him.

"You're not serious?"

"Da."

"No." She pulled back from the comfort of his arms, resting her hands lightly on his chest. Oh, how she loved to touch him. "This is Australia--we don't kill people here, even if they are a slimy, blackmailing bastards."

"He be threat to you because of me. You my voman, I vill not allow."

His words brought a warm smile to her lips. She loved it when he called her *his* woman. An idea started to formulate in her mind.

"They way I see it right now, legally you don't have a leg to stand on. If the authorities learn of how you came to be in Australia then, no doubt, you'll be put into detention, maybe even get deported. But I won't allow that to happen. I've got money, and you've come from a really bad situation. We're going to go to Melbourne, and I'm going to pull every string I can to make you a legal resident of Australia. That way, worms like Leeman can keep squirming in the muck they came from and we can keep you safe from those who murdered your people."

He folded his arms, and his expression was one of serious stubbornness. He was a proud man; she could understand how hard it may be for him to accept this--especially coming from her.

"I no take money from you."

She raised an eyebrow at him. He was going to learn she could be just as stubborn as him.

"This isn't about money. This is about doing the right thing; so don't let your stubborn pride get in the way. I don't care much for money either, but right now it's going to come in damn handy. I need you to put your trust in me. No more hiding. And if you're bogged down over the finances, then we'll call it a loan, and you can pay me back. So, will you do that? Trust me to take care of this--and you?"

He looked like he was spoiling for a fight. She could almost see the cogs working in his mind, trying to figure out other possible solutions, which would not allow her the opportunity to help him as she wanted to.

"I should be taking care of you," he grumbled, making her want to smile at his macho male attitude. And in a way, it was very sweet.

He moved suddenly, taking her by surprise as he grabbed her upper arms and pulled her back against his body. Her head tilted back as she gazed up into his intense pale depths.

"My fierce *krasIvaya*, you like tigress. Make me very proud. I vill trust, and I vill pay debt."

His mouth crashed down over hers. She wrapped her arms around his neck and kissed him back with the same heated passion.

He pulled back, and it forced her to take in several deep breaths to calm her suddenly ragged breathing.

Damn, what the man could do to her with a simple kiss. She forced herself to concentrate and get her mind off jumping Mohan's bones.

"We'd better make a move. I want to be in Melbourne before the night is through. I'll go pack a few things."

He released her from his arms, and she gave him what she hoped was a comforting smile before turning away.

It was then she noticed the flicker of a candle atop a new table where her foldable camping table had once sat. The smell of cooked food mixed with new timber varnish penetrated her senses. She had been too caught up with worry to notice her surroundings. She stopped dead in her tracks and stared at the table and the place settings.

Silence hung in the room as she stepped forward and gently touched the table with the tips of her fingers, realizing this was the large piece of felled tree Mohan had been working on in the shed.

It didn't have smooth, symmetrical sides but followed the natural roundness of the tree from which it had been cut. The rich grain of the timber was enhanced by the timber polish he had used. It fit perfectly into the dining area of the house and added to the rough, natural beauty of their home.

It was a more a work of art than a table. Julia was at a loss for words. She was unable to prevent tears from sliding down her cheeks.

"You no like table?"

His blurred, worried face came into view.

She swiped at her tears with the back of her hands and threw her arm around him.

"I love it! It is the most beautiful table I've ever seen. I'm just so touched you have done this for me."

He let out a breath of what seemed to be relief at her words, and she could not help but give a small chuckle. "You are the most amazing, talented man I know. I-lo…" she stumbled on the last two words.

Most men ran at the sound of the 'l' word. It was opening a whole new level of vulnerability if she confessed her love for him and he could not or would not reciprocate.

It was better to focus on one thing at a time. "Thank you, Mohan. When this is over and you're safely an Aussie resident, we'll come back to celebrate."

"Da, sound good. I bring Vodka." He flashed a megawatt grin.

"It's a deal. C'mon, let's hurry." Her own goofy grin fell as she suddenly remembered Mo.

"Oh damn! What about Mo? It's not as if I can ask any old neighbour to feed him, nor can we take him with us."

That same strange look of irritation flashed across Mohan's face. Julia was starting to get the impression he did not like her tiger.

"He big cat. Take care of himself before you come, vill be fine vithout you." He suddenly spun her around his arms and pushed her towards the bedroom. "You say you need to pack, so go pack, voman. Ve make haste, da?"

He was right. Mo was surviving without her before she arrived. She only hoped he would still be around when they got back.

Chapter Fourteen

As much as he hated to admit it, Julia was right. Running and hiding the way he had was no way to live. If he was going to make her a permanent part of his life, then he needed to do things the legal way. He did not know much about how Australians conducted their legal affairs, but he was about to find out.

He was annoyed with the fact she had not understood what he was trying to tell her just before their tryst in the shed. It was one thing to accept he had stripe birthmarks, but he was still uncertain how she would react if he shifted in front of her.

Despite he and his tiger being one, he was starting to feel rather jealous of the fact she had confessed her love to his tiger.

Give it time, he chided himself. *Make her fall in love with you first. Then, when the time comes, reveal the truth.* He prayed to the gods she would accept both man and beast.

In his younger days, Mohan had travelled extensively around Europe. He had seen the lights of many cities, but seeing the multitude of lights spread out across this city of Melbourne brought a sense of wonder mixed with foreboding, a feeling of being trapped. So many people. Although he did not need to shift, he enjoyed the freedom of loosing his beast. Being in tiger form also gave him strength and enhanced senses. It was why his kind always returned to the safety of the village after roaming the world.

The drive was long, and Julia was tired. He kept her talking, asking questions about her childhood. Every word he spoke helped towards improving his English skills, and he enjoyed listening to the soft husky sound of her voice. It soothed him and helped him learn more about his woman.

Julia was an only child. It seemed to him she had a lonely life, as both parents were too busy to pay much attention to her. She spoke more fondly of the woman paid to care for her than she did her mother. Her father she clearly adored. He had died from heart failure not long after Julia's marriage to a man who was only after what he could get from her father, not from her.

She was a tender heart, which was just one of many things he treasured about her, and he was amazed at how untainted she was by the wealth of her family. She had a compassionate, caring nature, which she demonstrated time and time again in wanting to help him and care for the tiger. No doubt this nature had been exploited by those around her, but she had shown a growing strength and an ability to stand up for herself. No doubt a result of too many people walking over her. It was something he would not allow while she was in his care.

"Vhy did you stay vith this man so long vhen you knew he vas unfaithful?"

"Hope, I suppose," she said thoughtfully, her eyes fixed on the road as she navigated the modern, lamp lit streets. They had come into an area with more opulent houses than the ones he had observed in the outer fringes of the city. "Hope Richard would not do it again, hope I could make my marriage work. I was a fool to have put up with it for so long."

"You are strong voman, no fool. He be fool for do such things to you. I no fool." He leaned over, placing his hand over hers where it rested near her thigh. He felt bereft when he went too long without some kind of contact with her.

She glanced at him briefly, a smile in her tired gaze. "No, I know you are no fool. We'll get this all sorted out."

It grated against his grain to allow her to do this, yet he knew it was necessary. A woman should not be fighting his battles. It was not the way he was brought up. Even from an early cub, Mohan had been taught women were to be cherished and provided for. In turn, they cared for their men, took care of the children and home, and provided a warm, nurturing atmosphere. It made a man proud to work hard for his woman and provide for her.

In this land, she held all the wealth--and his future--in her small hands. What made it all right was the trust and faith he had in her, knowing he would one day return the favour.

In every other aspect, he would watch over and care for her. She was his, after all.

Single shifter females were rare among his people. Even though the women did birth multiple cubs at a time, to have female cubs was a rare treasure. He wondered if Julia, being human, would conceive more than one.

"Vhy you have no children?" His question seemed to startle her. She gave him a sharp glance. He saw a sudden, painful expression cross her face.

"It never came up." From the pitch of her voice, he knew she was lying.

"Tell truth, Julia," he ordered firmly.

She was silent for a moment before answering. "Richard didn't want children. I did, desperately. Not once during our marriage did I take or use any kind of contraceptive. If I was able to get pregnant, then I would have. I think I know what you're thinking. We didn't use protection while having sex; it was stupid I know, but you can't get me pregnant, if that what's worrying you."

"I vant you to have my cubs," he stated in all seriousness. There was no reason to hide that fact from her.

Mohan had to quickly reach for the wheel of the car, jerking it back onto the road when she almost drove into a lamppost.

She slowed the car and was silent for a long moment. Her eyes stayed fixed on the road and both hands gripped the steering wheel tightly.

"Hold that thought," she muttered under her breath as she turned into another street. He wished he knew what she was thinking.

The car turned into a driveway. She brought them to a halt outside a large, double story, blue stone house. She yanked on the park break and turned off the engine before giving him her full attention.

"Cubs? You mean kids," she finally spoke.

"Da, a litter."

"You really take this tiger stuff seriously." She stared at him in bemusement. "Mohan, I can't conceive. You've picked the wrong woman if you want a family."

He could tell she was trying to keep the bitterness from her tone, but he was not as convinced of the fact she could not have children as she was. Time would soon tell, and there was one sure way of knowing. He would have to taste her in his tiger form.

"No. I choose perfect voman for me. It no matter. I still vant you, Julia, cubs or no."

The expression of utter adoration in her eyes only confirmed he had made the right choice. "Dis be your home?"

She blinked in confusion before turning her head and glancing out the window to the darkened house.

"Yes, my family home. My mother lives in an apartment in the city. Dad left everything to me. And I made Richard move out, so I guess it's our home now."

Anywhere with this woman was home now, and he needed to take care of her.

"You are tired. Come, lead vay to bed. Ve sleep."

~ * ~

Julia had never cared much for jeans, but watching Mohan move as the dark blue material covered his powerful legs and encased the best ass she'd ever laid eyes on made her wanted to bow down and worship the makers of Levis.

Earlier that morning, he had argued with her about buying him more clothes, but she had won due to the fact they were on their way to meet her solicitor, Raewin Macintire. She did not want him looking like he had just walked off a building site.

The six-foot-tall woman solicitor had a reputation as one of the finest legal minds in Melbourne.

Raewin was like a pit bull--once she sank her teeth into something, she did not let go until she won the day. It was exactly who she and Mohan needed on their side.

Julia had left Raewin an urgent message on her phone late the night before--before Mohan put her to bed. With his warm, secure arms wrapped around her, it didn't take long for Julia to fall into a blissful sleep.

The beeping of Julia's phone awoke them a few hours later. Raewin had called her back, telling her to bring Mohan into her office just before ten. Especially since Julia had explained how someone had tried to blackmail her.

Mohan strode from the dressing room, ignoring the saleswoman who had been hovering--and drooling--over him since he had walked in.

Jealousy was not the only thing making Julia's teeth grind, but the fact was, there were many prettier and younger women who could draw his attention. It was an ever-present fear Mohan would turn out just like Richard, only using her for what he could get.

To her relief, he did not seem interested and shoved off any attempt the saleswoman made to engage him in conversation. In fact, he ignored the woman almost to the point of rudeness, forcing her to go through Julia whenever she needed to ask a question.

"Look good, da?" he asked with an impish smile.

"Da, very handsome." Julia swallowed, loving the way the fitted T-shirt and the dark brown leather jacket hung on his body and enhanced his overall masculinity. Not overly dressy, but not underdressed either. Mind you, she had seen him in rags, and he looked damn good no matter what he wore.

He leaned down and kissed her boldly in front of the saleswoman. Julia was not accustomed to public displays of affection. Richard always told her it should be kept behind closed doors.

Mohan was open, passionate, and did not seem to care who saw them.

"We'd better go," she murmured huskily when he pulled back.

"Da, ve not keep the lavyer vating."

She gave him another goofy grin and nodded.

"Ring up what he's wearing, and can you bag his other clothes? Thank you," Julia ordered the sales lady, who was still gazing at them with envy.

Let them look, she thought with possessive pride. At the end of the day, Mohan was her man.

~ * ~

John Leeman was seething. Julia Cooper had not shown up. Fuming, he had driven all the way out to her house, only to find the place empty. She had bolted with her boy toy. John was going to make her pay, one-way or the other.

On the drive back to the real estate office, he racked his brain, trying to come up with a way to bring Julia and her lover down. Once inside his office, he kept the *Closed* sign on and slumped angrily down into his office chair. The only way he could think to hurt her was to tear the lover boy from her. He was about to look up the phone number to the immigration department when a flashing icon at the bottom of his computer screen told him his search results for Julia's Russian man had come back positive.

He clicked on the icon and found a message and a photo waiting for him. The photo was a side image of the same man who he watched fucking Julia Cooper.

Curious, he read the attached message. His anger suddenly drained as he sat back in his seat and smiled. This may just work out even better than trying to blackmail the elusive Julia Cooper.

Leeman leaned forward and typed a response. Payday and revenge were just around the corner, all thanks to one freaky Russian man.

Chapter Fifteen

Bill Ashcroft steepled his fingers and tapped his chin with them as he leaned back in his plush, black leather office chair, thinking over the information he had just received from Australia.

It seemed he had found his stray cat.

It had been too risky to fly the sole survivor of his hunt to his compound in the southwest United States. Instead, he had used one of his ships to export this new, prized possession across the ocean. It was a less-risky way of transporting his rarest treasures.

Hunting was his passion. Killing a creature more powerful than he was a thrill he had become addicted too. He was always seeking out a new adventure and a new predator to add to his collection.

When you had as much money as he did, nothing was off limits. People were always willing to look the other way when the right amount greased their palms.

This time it has been the endangered white Siberian tiger in the remote coniferous forests of eastern Russia. Four days into his trip, he had opted to explore a rather dense and almost-hidden valley set between two mountain ranges. He and his guide had been surprised to stumble across a small village.

The overly paid guide had informed Ashcroft he had only ever heard rumours about the hidden village. He had heard the people were supposed to possess the spirits of both man and beast. They were unnatural, dangerous, and to be avoided at all cost.

Bill Ashcroft was not one to be frightened away by superstitions, but he also knew many rumours were founded in fact. These people had gone to great lengths to keep their small township hidden away from the rest of the world--leaving Bill very curious.

Staying out of the way, he had set up hidden telescopic cameras to observe the main center of the village. Then he left the village in peace for several days before returning to collect the footage.

What he had discovered was priceless. At first he wondered why the men and a few women went about nearly naked. He had assumed the tiger-striped tattoos all over their bodies were some kind of tribal symbol, but he soon found out why they had the markings. Before his very eyes, he saw them transform into white tigers.

The markings were not tattoos at all. They were reflections of exactly what these people were--shape shifters.

It had taken him a whole day to contemplate the implications of his discovery. They were not men, nor were they tigers. They were both.

They were unknown and unrecognized by any government or body of law--hence, they were a new huntable species.

The thought made him giddy. Since man was the top predator on the planet, these would come in a high second; the intelligence of man and the mystery of the beast.

It was not just a hunt and a kill. Beyond that, he wanted to take one for a prize to keep in his little zoo of exotic creatures.

Finding armed mercenaries was very easy in Russia. He made plans and set traps, surrounding the area to make sure there would be no possible way of escape. After all, he would not want to leave any witnesses to what they were about to do.

He wanted a couple of tiger men in cages. Ivan, his top, right hand man, was to make sure the other men knew not to kill everything. He wanted his cages full.

Unfortunately, his orders had either been lost in translation or they did not care, because by the time the dust settled on the village raid, practically everything had been wiped out. Bill was furious. What was he going to hunt now? He had been surprised by the way the tiger women had killed their own children rather than let them be taken.

It was the males who put up the most vicious fight and refused to surrender. Afterward, he and his men had picked through the bodies and found one still alive. They quickly caged him and shipped him out before anyone came across the carnage of the village.

And now, he had nothing. The idiot placed in charge of feeding the creature had been careless. The tiger had torn out the man's throat before making a dash through the ship and jumping overboard.

He knew the only country within rage of the ship when the tiger man had jumped was Australia, but he had not known if the tiger man had survived--until now.

He had put his best computer tech on the job to carefully place Internet feelers out into the global network, trying to find any hint of a strangely striped, tattooed man or out of place white Siberian tigers.

Sure enough, one curious real estate agent had found just that, a striped, tattooed man living in the state of Victoria in Australia.

To make sure, Bill had sent an image of the man from his camera, only to get a positive response. He had sneered when he saw the man had attached a price tag to his information, but it did not matter. A shape shifter tiger was certainly worth the small sum this measly man was asking.

Mohan, the man had called him. The creature's name amused him. How would a remote Siberian village know of the famed Indian tiger named by an Indian prince back in the 1820s?

Again, it did not matter. Bill was going to reclaim the man tiger and put it exactly where it had been destined to be--in his cages.

Bill leaned forward and snatched up his phone. "Captain Hammerick, prepare the ship for a new trip. We're going to Australia. I have a lost acquisition to reacquire."

~ * ~

"She be scary voman," Mohan said, placing the shopping bags down on the kitchen counter.

Julia smiled as she grabbed the bag, removing the perishables and placing them in the tall, shiny fridge freezer.

"Raewin is a marvel to behold and will work hard to make things right for you."

Her heart had gone out to him as she sat and listened to him recount his story in detail to Raewin.

Raewin had assured him the massacre of his people was grounds alone to be offered safe haven in Australia. Raewin had political contacts in immigration and would see to it personally that he was granted special consideration for asylum due to what he had suffered.

She was also going to contact the Russian embassy and have someone look into the massacre. It was a crime that should not go unpunished. Although Mohan was unsure of exactly who had committed the violence, he gave Raewin names and descriptions of the men he had seen and heard during his captivity.

Julia had not said anything, but she stayed by his side, holding his hand. She gave him silent assurance that, no matter the outcome, he was safe and she would stand by his side.

"It's going to take some time, but identity papers and the immigration papers should be done within two weeks. And trust me,"

Raewin had assured them before they left her offices later that day, "that is as fast as I can make them go."

Julia, without hesitation, had put her name down as his Australian sponsor.

Anything it took, Julia would do.

~ * ~

"You don't mind spending all this time here in Melbourne?"

Julia closed the fridge and turned around, only to encounter a wall of solid Mohan. He moved so damn silently. Her head tilted up, and she was startled by the raw hungry passion in his gaze as he backed her against the refrigerator door. He bent down to take her mouth with his, and her arms wrapped around his shoulders as he ravaged her. A low moan rose from her throat, and the world spun as oxygen became scarce. He pulled back, allowing her to breath once again.

"Every time I have you, I vant more," he breathed against her throat. He nuzzled into her skin before sucking at the sweet spot just at the junction of her neck and shoulders.

Julia was in a haze of erotic sensation. Liquid fire surged through her body.

"I never knew I could feel this way until you." Her voice was tight with need. She slid her fingers though Mohan's soft hair.

Already he had slipped his hands around to her waist and unzipped her grey pencil skirt, pushing it down her hips. She felt the material pool at her feet. She stepped out of it and kicked the material aside while he tugged up her black satin blouse. Her hands rose as he quickly pulled it off and tossed it aside. Her blouse joined the abandoned skirt on the kitchen floor, leaving her in black lace panties and bra.

"Da, my voman made for me. Soft, rounded. Mine. I love to taste." He demonstrated his love by laving at the skin of her throat. He dropped to his knees and ran his tongue over the flesh, dipping it into her belly button and making her giggle. The laughter swiftly turned into a moan as his other hand pushed aside the fabric of her panties. His fingers parted the fold of her wet inner flesh.

The pressure of his finger on her swollen clit made her arch back against the cool of the fridge door. She barely registered the tug that ripped her panties and exposed her fully to his gaze, and so much more.

"You like tiger licking?"

Julia could only assume he was referring to himself as a tiger again. It was a bit crazy, but at this point, she really did not care. She was hot, horny, and wanted Mohan.

"Yes." She let out on a long moan as his fingers moved in firm circles on her swollen nub. "I love it when you lick me. Please, Mohan, please."

Mohan heeded her call, throwing her legs over his strong shoulders and burying his face between her legs. She grappled in desperation for something her hand could grip onto, a sudden whirring and loud clunking penetrated through her lust-drunk brain. She turned her head to see she had hit the ice dispenser on the fridge door. Ice scattered in all directions across the kitchen floor.

Mohan chuckled into the fold of her sex. He pulled his head back and glanced around. Julia met his gaze, and a wicked grin spread across his face.

"You like ice?"

Her eyes widened as he picked up a cube and popped it into his mouth. Then he once again buried his face between her legs.

Her shriek pierced the air as the ice touched her clit. Then his hot wet tongue replaced the ice and sucked away the cold. He gripped her hips in his hand and continued to use the ice, placing it against her clit as he sucked on it with long, hard pulls.

It was literally fire and ice between her legs. The dual sensation of the heat and cold made her writhe and moan until her keening cry filled the kitchen. Her body flushed crimson as she came hard. Her breathing was short and choppy as Mohan released her from his mouth and rose to his feet, licking his lips.

Julia simply stared at him in awe. From his impassioned gaze, she knew he was far from finished with her. He lifted her, and she wrapped her legs around his waist. He pinned her soft body with his hard one. His cock found the mouth of her sex. He thrust his hips and embedded himself deeply within her.

Her inner walls, still clenching with her climax, were now forced open by the sudden intrusion of his cock. She moaned with intense pleasure.

Weak from the massive clitoral climax he had just given her, all she could do was cling helplessly to him as he pounded into her. He changed the angle of his thrusts and hit her internal pleasure button at just the right angle, over and over. The refrigerator thumped against the wall every time he speared into her.

It was useless. She felt the pressure building up within as she panted and made small mewling sounds. She held on tightly.

Her body shook as he pushed her to the brink then over. Crying out his name, her world exploded into pure bliss.

Mohan growled low, and she felt him shake feverously. His thrusts became jerky until he thrust one last time and held still as he came.

They held on to each other. Their heaving chests and sweaty bodies slowly started to calm from the euphoric bliss. Julia lifted her head from Mohan's shoulder and gazed into his beautiful pale depths.

She could not keep the satisfied smile from her lips. "Surely sex can't get any better than that?"

He gave her a cocky grin. "Vith us, *krasIvaya,* it can only get better."

Julia giggled. Then she moaned in disappointment as he pulled from her. Her legs felt like rubber as her feet, still clad in heels, touched the floor. She had to lock her knees together and use the fridge for support to stop her body from sliding to the floor.

"Soon, be time for you to know tiger as vell as man. Soon I show you truth. I try, but you will see, and you believe. No be frightened."

Well that was as cryptic as it got. Her brows knitted together in confusion. Why did he keep referring back to Mo? Or was it his tiger worshiping people? Just because he had striped birthmarks, it didn't make him an actual tiger. The possibility Mohan was simply being crazy…well, she did not want to contemplate that.

"I don't understand what you're talking about."

He leaned in to give her a woefully brief kiss. "Soon you vill. Hurry, dress. I hear somevone at door."

She watched him stride out, pulling up his jeans as he went. She was irritated he had not even undressed again, and here she was, standing around in only her bra.

Startled by the sound of the doorbell chiming through the house, she quickly scrambled to find and pull on her clothes.

~ * ~

"You haven't been answering my calls, young lady."

It was a damn good thing Julia was still enjoying her post sexual bliss, or the sudden tension she felt creeping into her shoulders would have been a hell of a lot worse.

"Nice to see you to, Mum," Julia muttered as Lexi Lancaster pushed past her into the house. She swiveled on her expensive six-inch heels.

For a woman her age, trying to dress like a twenty-year-old fashion model just did not work. Her hair was a bleached blond, her leopard-patterned, skin-tight dress hugged her bony body, and Julia had no idea which parts were still original.

Her face appeared younger than her age, but it also had an unnatural shine--evidence of her obsession with plastic surgery and always trying to look younger.

Her mother pushed back her sunglasses and glanced over her daughter in a critical manner--a look Julia had always hated.

"Your top is askew, there is a large hicky on your neck, and your hair is frizzed up. Needless to say, you've got the hallmarks of someone who's just had sex. Done the smart thing at last and taken Richard back?"

"No, Mum, I haven't. And who I have sex with is none of your business." Julia had not let go of the door handle. Her grip tightened around it.

"Richard isn't going to be happy about you screwing around on him."

"We are divorced. He is a past mistake I never want to repeat again, so you can stop it, Mother. I will never take Richard back. I am involved with someone else--someone I care very deeply for."

Lexi gave a disbelieving snort and rolled her eyes. She strode deeper into the house, forcing Julia to close the door and follow after her mother. Julia resisted the urge to grind her teeth.

Her mother's tone and expression were condescending as she gave an exaggerated sigh of exasperation. "Perhaps I did shelter you too much as a child. Everyone needs to get out and sow their wild oats. I guess you're just making up for lost time. No matter. Once you're done playing around, I am sure Richard will understand. He told me himself he's missing you terribly."

Julia was on the verge of boiling over. "Why are you so damn obsessed with me getting back together with Richard? If you want him so badly, then you go fuck the bastard. After all, I'm sure there isn't one woman out there he hasn't fucked!"

Lexi folded her arms. "Don't take that tone with me, young lady. I am still your mother and deserve some respect. If you had been more open sexually, then he wouldn't have needed to have those other liaisons."

Just like always, her mother thought she could bully and intimidate her, but not this time. She would not be baited by her mother, so she ignored the last nasty remark.

"Why are you here?" Julia folded her arms defensively across her chest.

"I heard you'd come back from that old dump of your grandfather's. Richard asked me to come and try to talk some sense into you." Lexi had entered one of the sitting rooms and headed towards the bar. It was well stocked with an assortment of alcohol left over from Richard's taste for hard liquor.

Julia felt a stress headache coming on at the front of her skull. She watched Lexi help herself to a vodka and tonic. Julia stood tensely by the door watching her.

"What he wants is for me to hand him Lancaster Exports. You know I received the majority of the share holdings in the divorce. And if he ever came near me again, I would sell my shares to an overseas investor."

"How can you be so heartless to a man who obviously still loves you?"

It was Julia's turn to give an unladylike snort. "You can forget it, Mother. Richard can to go hell for all I care."

"Julia… " Her mother's tone held a note of warning. Lexi raised her glass to her glossy red lips, but the glass hovered as something behind Julia caught Lexi's attention.

Julia felt Mohan's heat at her back before his large hand glided around her waist. She turned her head and gazed into Mohan's pale depths.

"Mohan, this is my mother, Lexi Lancaster." Julia did not even bother to look at her mother as she made the introduction. Just having Mohan by her side strengthened her resolve and drained the tension from her body.

"She no look like you," Mohan commented. His gaze swept over Julia's mother, who, started to preen under his appraisal. "Julia more beautiful," he declared, making Lexi scowl and Julia grin like an idiot. Julia had to hold back her giggle when Mohan asked, "Why your mother look like shiny old doll?"

Lexi now glared daggers at Mohan.

"Slumming it with Russian's now, Julia? I once assumed you had class when you married Richard, but clearly I was wrong."

Julia turned her attention and fury to her mother. "You come into my home and insult me in every possible manner as you do other people's dirty work. But insulting Mohan is the last straw. I suggest you leave peacefully now, or I will throw you out on your ear."

Although Julia kept her tone calm, it dripped with menace. Mother or not, she was through with putting up with bitchy, pushy people who thought they could walk all over her.

"This was once my home. Your no good father--"

"Don't you dare say anything against Dad. And you wonder why Dad left everything to me! Because he knew you were always self-centered and self-serving. I love you, Mum, but I won't put up with your crap anymore. Now leave. I won't ask you a second time."

It did not take long for her mother to realize Julia was not going to relent. She gave a huff. "Fine way to treat the mother who birthed you and raised you," she snidely remarked as she walked past them with her head held high.

"I would hardly call what you did 'raising a child,'" Julia threw back at her, making sure her mother kept heading towards the door.

Lexi paused, her dark blue eyes cold as she stared at Julia. She opened her mouth as if to say something but shut it again.

With Mohan still by Julia's side, she watched as Lexi climbed into her Mercedes and sped off.

Julia let out a breath of relief.

"Pray she never comes back." Julia turned to Mohan. He closed the front door and locked it as they walked back inside.

"Hard to believe she be your mother. Vhy is her face like that?"

"Plastic surgery. Every inch of her skin has been poked, prodded at, tightened, and who knows what else, in an attempt to make her look younger."

"It no work. She still look old."

Julia grinned at him.

"You very sexy when angry." He gave her a seductive grin and sent her pulse into hyper-drive as he stepped in closer.

Julia licked her lips. "You think so?" She ran her hands up and over his torso. Finding the hem of his shirt, she tugged it up to touch his naked skin.

"Da, but I think you sexy all time."

"Well, that we have in common. I think you're sexy as hell too."

"Da, you have told me." He was walking her backwards towards the stairs. His fingers found the hem of her shirt. "Dis better off than on."

"Same with you, big boy. I love the way you look without clothes on. And after that encounter with the wicked mother of the west, I am in definite need of cheering up. Think you can handle that?"

"Da. Easy."

Julia was in a playful mood. She pulled away just before he bent down to kiss her. Mohan let out a low growl as she spun on her heel and darted up the stairs. "Catch me first, big boy."

She gave a shriek of laughter as Mohan gave chase. He caught her at the doorway of the bedroom. Mohan kicked the door shut behind them.

Chapter Sixteen

Mohan was restless, and his tiger even more so. Eight days had passed since he had last shifted. Soon he would need to loose his tiger for a while.

The immigration authorities alerted to his presence had come to see him, but Julia had made sure Raewin would be present through all meetings. They asked him the same questions but in different ways. He could see they were trying to trip him up, to prove he was not who or what he said he was.

But he never wavered. You could not trip up if the truth was all you could tell. Hiding the fact he was a tiger was not even an issue--considering they would simply think him mad.

They had left him with a lot of paperwork to fill in, but Raewin was also helping in that department. Julia smiled with delight when she realized he could read as well as write English.

"A man full of talents." She had placed her hands under her chin, gazing provocatively at him. It was more than he could stand. Needless to say, they had to set everything in the office back in order once he had finished fucking her on the desk, but when she had bent over to retrieve her shredded clothes, he had taken her over the chair.

Julia was his solace and his peace. His need for her was ever-growing. Taking his pleasure in her soft body, listening to the way she called his name over and over--he knew he could never have enough of this beautiful, giving woman.

And he gave back all he could in attention and care. They took long walks in the surrounding parklands of her home. He had been forbidden to leave the city, due to the fact he still had no identity papers.

On the tenth day, a knock came at the door. He was playing chess with Julia in one of the sitting rooms. She rose and left the room to answer the door as he studied the board for his next move.

Hearing more than one man's voice, he abandoned the game to make sure the visitors were of the friendly type.

Hearing a Russian accent put him on alert. He came to stand protectively behind Julia.

"Mohan, these men claim to be from the Russian Embassy in Canberra."

"May we come in?" a short, pudgy man asked in fluent Russian. He had dark eyes and short-cropped, plain brown hair. "We've come to ask you about the crime near the town of *Verkh Gorin* you have reported."

Julia glanced from Mohan to the two men.

"It is all right, Julia. Let them in." He kept his tone calm, not wanting her to worry.

Trustingly, she stepped back. Mohan switched to speaking Russian. "Come this way."

He led them into the study. Julia hovered by the door. He could see she was tense and worried. He gave her a reassuring smile and a brief kiss on the cheek.

"I am sure the gentlemen would like some refreshments. Some tea?"

She gave a nod, turned, and left the three of them together.

"I am Anton. This is my colleague, Boris. We are from the investigations bureau in Russia. When your story passed our desk, we quickly contacted our people in western Russia and had them investigate the allegation." Anton had shot straight to the point. He sat down and opened a black leather briefcase.

"First, we have had your papers sent to us. Your passport, although no longer valid, has been reissued." He handed Mohan a new Russian passport. Mohan took it, flipping it open to find it had also been stamped with Australian stamps.

"But what was more disturbing is we found evidence of what you described. You said your people protected the tiger population of the Amur region?"

"Yes. We have worked with the park rangers. As we have always had a kinship with the animals, we always tried to protect them. The American and his men murdered my family and friends to get to the tigers," Mohan said bitterly.

Next to emerge from Anton's case were a dozen or so photographs. Mohan swallowed as he took them. He stared down at the black-and-white images of burnt-out houses he had helped build, the decomposing bodies of tigers he knew as friends. Most of the village had shifted into tigers when the attack began, hoping to outrun or fight off the attackers.

It was well known whatever skin you died in was the form you stayed in. No one would ever know they were a clan of shape shifting tigers. No more ridicule or investigation into what they were would ever be done. Even if it was animals, what kind of person massacred a famously protected species such as this?

A wave of dizziness swept over him. His hand trembled in anger and grief as fresh memories of that night came flooding back, images from before he had been knocked out and awoken in a cage. Blindly, he shoved the images back to Anton.

He sank down into a nearby chair. "I am to assume this was your village."

"Yes," Mohan said tightly. "We are different, but there was no need to kill us for it."

"Why did you survive?" The one named Boris spoke for the first time.

"I was knocked out in the midst of fighting them. There were just too many, and too many guns."

"We found American guns and bullet casings all over the area. You say that Bill Ashcroft is responsible for the massacre?"

Helplessness swept over him, adding to his tumultuous rage. He had been over it a thousand times in his mind. What could he have done to stop it? And every time it was the same answer--nothing. Who was he to read the fates and know that man would decide to destroy everything he had ever known?

Nor did he know the fates would deliver him to a land wherein lived a woman he could not conceivably live without.

"There is no place in hell good enough for that despicable dog. He took me and put me in a cage like an animal. If I had not escaped, I do not know what would have become of me."

Both of his fellow Russians gave short sharp nods of agreement.

"We have already found a few of the men he paid to hunt with him. They too confirmed it was Bill Ashcroft. We have issued a silent, Europe-wide warrant for his arrest. Unfortunately, he is safe and protected in America. But there is one thing about their stories I do not understand. All the men babble on about the village being full of tiger men. Do you know why this is?"

"We were all born with unique birthmarks," Mohan explained, rolling up the sleeve of his arm to reveal a part of the strips he bore. "These extend to most of our bodies. It is one of the reasons we feel a kinship with the tiger, and why we chose to live a life dedicated to protecting them."

It was all true. There were plenty of tigers that could not shift into a human form. Nor did he feel any guilt for telling half-truths. He had fed them enough truthful information without giving away the whole secret. Hiding one, final secret in plain sight was his only choice.

"This is a terrible tragedy that should have never occurred, but on behalf of Russian relations, I think it best if we kept this matter private. You will, of course, be compensated for your suffering. It was most fortunate you escaped to this fine country. I also see what a fine woman you have secured. It would be a shame to lose such fortunes now you have them."

Mohan knew what Anton was saying. The Russian government was going to pay him to keep his mouth shut about the killings and to let them handle things.

He did not want to lose Julia or for them to know the real truth. But it was also a weight off his shoulders he would not be forced to go back to Siberia.

"I will never forget the day that man came and murdered so many. You will continue to see he is brought to justice?"

"We can guarantee it, *Mohan Alexandrov.* This is a crime against mother Russia herself. Rest assured, you are safe. Our government and the Australian government have both agreed to arrest Bill Ashcroft if he ever steps foot in either of our countries."

"The papers and compensation will come soon. Go live a happy life. Marry your woman and have many babies," Anton said, as if trying to be a comfort. Anton and Boris rose to their feet just as Julia reappeared carrying a tray of tea.

"Thank you, gentlemen." Mohan had switched to English again. He took the tea tray from Julia's hands and set it down. She studied him carefully before slipping her hand into his and giving it a reassuring squeeze. Just her simple touch helped ease the anger and grief surrounding him.

"Thank you for helping, Mohan. Mrs Cooper, I wish you both much happiness."

Mohan had to hold back a growl as Anton paused, taking hold of Julia's free hand and lifting it to kiss the back of her fingers. Mohan did not like anyone touching his woman--nor did he like any scent on her but his.

"It has been my privilege, but thank you anyway," she said gracefully, removing her hand from Anton's grasp before gazing questioningly at Mohan.

Mohan took her hand and drew her away from the men. He slipped an arm around her waist and brought her close to his side as they walked the men out.

"Is everything all right?"

He pulled her into his arms and buried his face in the lavender scent of her hair. He drew strength and comfort from having her in his embrace. She anchored her arms around his waist, helping to calm the emotional turmoil he felt inside.

"Da, very soon it will be. My story has been confirmed by the Russian authorities. I am free man, free to live in Australia."

"That's wonderful news, but then why did you look so anguished?" She lifted her head and rested her chin on his chest.

Why? Because at first he thought there was nothing he wanted more than to rip out the throat of Bill Ashcroft. Gazing down into Julia's sweet deep-blue eyes, he had something he wanted even more--to keep his woman safe.

He may never forget what happened, but with Julia, he could move on and have a life free from persecution, free from men who would hunt him.

There was only one thing left to do. He and his tiger's future now hung on how she reacted to him revealing exactly what he was.

~ * ~

Julia was worried. He had been silent and brooding ever since the men from the Russian embassy had visited. He had shown her his new Russian passport, and, three days later, Raewin had presented Mohan with his permanent residency papers. Then they all went together to set him up with his own bank account.

"Some politicians moved heaven and Earth to get these through quickly," Raewin had informed them during her visit the next morning. Raewin's grin was triumphant, as she had once won the day again. "It's amazing what red tape people can cut through if motivated."

Julia was not stupid and understood some compromises must have been made. She knew Mohan enough to understand he was a private person--she doubted he would ever draw media attention to his plight.

Now that he had everything he needed, she knew he no longer needed her. Her anxiety grew when he insisted on paying back all she had spent on him in legal fees and clothing.

Two weeks to the day since they had come to Melbourne, Mohan, with a new driver's license in hand, asked to borrow her car. She smiled and nodded, jokingly telling him not to run too many people over. She had to fight back the impulse to ask him where he wanted to go and if she could go too. But he needed his space, and he had been with her for two weeks. No doubt he needed a break.

Mohan swung her up in his arms, kissing her deeply before taking the keys. Julia had a goofy smile on her face as she watched him stride out the door.

Her tension and fear grew as she heard the car start and pull away from the house. Looking for a way to keep busy, she searched online for Russian recipes to surprise him with at dinnertime.

By the time it grew dark, the beef *Khartcho* and *Gouryevskaya Kashaal* were sitting ready, along with the candles and place settings. The more wine she drank, the deeper she slipped into a world of depression and self-doubt.

He had left her for another woman--just like Richard, sitting in her car fucking someone younger and prettier and thinner than she was. He did not need nor want her anymore. She had been nothing but a means to an end.

Anger curled through her as she drunkenly rose from the table and snatched the bottle of wine. She stumbled slightly as she wandered into the living room to sulk. She flopped down onto the sofa, drank another glass--and waited.

~ * ~

"How long you been sitting here like dis?"

Julia blinked when Mohan switched on the light. She glared up at him.

"Bloody long enough." She shoved to her feet. A glance at the clock told her it was just past midnight.

"Enjoy your time out?" she sneered. "Find the company you were looking for."

Confusion knitted his brow together.

"I get lost in Melbourne, until I find map on backseat. I saw dinner. Am very sorry, Julia. I still hungry."

"You're sorry!" She had to stop herself from actually screaming at him as the pain sliced though her. Richard always came home with lies and excuses. Now Mohan was doing the same damn thing!

"It was bad enough listening to Richard's lies, but I won't put up with any from you."

He simply raised a disbelieving eyebrow as she pushed passed him and up headed up the stairs.

"I no lie to you. I go to find place to let tiger run free," he said calmly, following closely on her heels.

Julia halted. She spun around, almost tripping over, but Mohan reached out to steady her. She shrugged him off and backed further up the stairs.

"Don't touch me! Maybe I was wrong, and you are crazy. You and this 'I am a tiger' shit. Wake up, Mohan! You are not a tiger! I don't want to hear any more excuses or lies. I've heard enough to last me two damn lifetimes."

Mohan looked angry and irritated, but she did not care.

"Julia, I have never…"

"Don't even try it, buddy," she cut him off. "Stay away from me! Go sleep in the guest room, because you're no longer welcome in my bed. As for tomorrow, you can pack your things and leave."

She ran the rest of the way to her bedroom, wincing as the door slammed behind her. She flung herself onto the bed and sobbed into the pillow. She loved Mohan with all her heart, and right now, it was being torn in two by his lies. He had sworn never to hurt her, and here he was doing just that.

~ * ~

Damn stubborn woman. Mohan stared at the closed door, debating whether he should barge in and set things straight. The woman had issues with trust. He understood, and getting lost in Melbourne had not been on his list of things he had wanted to do that afternoon. But talking to Raewin about a marriage license was one of them, and the second was finding a secluded Australian bushland in order to let his tiger loose and run free.

Mohan backed away from the door; it was time to confront her with the real truth. He had been doing his best to prepare her. He loved Julia with every inch of his heart and soul--there was no way he was going to lose her now.

He would give her time to calm down, time to rest. He needed time to stalk his prey and pounce. This time he would let his tiger free to do as he liked.

Chapter Seventeen

Excitement made her heart race and the blood pulsate through her veins in a heady rush. She squirmed under the delightful sensations of a wet, slightly raspy tongue pushing into her wet heat and rubbing against her clit, drifting between total awareness and the dream induced delight of Mohan between her thighs.

Good god, how she loved Mohan's tongue and the things he did to her body. Even in her sleep and desire-drunk brain she could not stop wanting, needing him. He brought fourth such vivid dreams.

Gasping, she dragged her legs up and planted her feet, splaying her thighs wider still. Weight settled on her thighs and pressed them deeper into the mattress as the mind tantalizing pleasure grew more intense. Her fingers reached out, searching for and finding the soft silken hair of the man between her thighs.

The pressure on her thighs dragged her up towards the precipice of consciousness, yet she was too enraptured by the wonderful sensations befuddling her brain to care.

She wanted the pleasure, wanted Mohan to finish and the dream to never end. Digging her fingers into his scalp, she lifted her hips to meet his insistent tongue. He lapped harder, pushing her closer and closer to release, until she was moaning incessantly, twisting her head back and forth against her pillow.

Her breath hitched, her body seized, and the first spasm jolted through her. Feeling the tremors of release flowing through her, he ceased to lick her clit pushing his tongue deep into her channel, tongue fucking her.

A cry tore from her lips as the muscles along her passage clenched so hard, her belly cramped and made her cry out again. She bucked against him until the spasms began, slowly, to fade.

She lay limply in the aftermath of her explosive climax. Julia gasped for breath.

"Oh, Mohan."

Any angry words from last night faded in a haze of sated bliss. How could she remain angry at Mohan? Perhaps she had been too hard on him. She had to consider the possibility he was telling the truth.

A deep purring made her crack open an eyelid. There sat Mo, his pale blue eyes blinking at her as his tongue licked his tiger lips. She pushed herself up onto her elbows and stared in disbelief. Yes, it was Mo, right there on her bed staring back. She squeezed her eyes shut then opened them again.

He most definitely was not a dream. And that tongue! His pink tongue that had just brought her to a mind-shattering climax.

"Oh, my god… What the hell?!"

She glanced down to see her nightgown bunched up around her waist. Her panties had been shredded by Mo's sharp teeth.

The tiger rose up on all fours. Julia's eyes widened as he stalked forward and forced her onto her back. The beast loomed over her. She fought back a sudden rise of panic, staring up into the tiger's piercing blue eyes.

"Mo…down, boy. Be a nice kitty now," she squeaked in fear.

Then it happened. Fur receded into flesh, and paws into hands and feet. The tiger face morphed into one she knew well. His shoulder length dark hair hung around his shoulders; he had tiger-striped markings echoing the pattern on Mo's body.

She had to know if he was real--if what she had just witnessed was real.

Trembling, she raised her hand and pressed it against his wall of firm, warm flesh.

"You tremble. Do not fear me. I tell you ve are vone, tiger and I."

Yes, he had been trying to tell her this all along, ever since the time in her grandfather's work shed.

Her perfect world of sense and reality crashed in around her. A cold sweat broke out across her body. Her stomach churned.

"Mohan, please let me up."

Worry etched into his features as he backed off her and the bed. Julia rolled over as the bile rose in her throat; she scrambled off the bed, making a mad dash towards the bathroom.

Her knees folded under her as she slumped over the open toilet bowl and heaved. In the background, she could hear water running. Then gentle hands brushed back her hair, and a cool damp cloth rested on the back of her neck.

Julia gripped the ceramic bowl tightly until she no longer felt the need to heave. Mohan pulled her away from the toilet and cleaned her face. He handed her a glass of water.

Still shaking, she accepted the glass and took small sips to rinse out her mouth, spitting the water back into the bowl after each sip. Finally, she let some of the cool, soothing liquid run down her dry throat.

"You are in shock. It vill pass soon."

Her stomach still felt unsettled, but at least not to the point of wanting to throw up again. Was it shock she was feeling? This was the real world she lived in, not some fantasyland where men could turn into tigers and tigers into men.

She lifted her gaze to meet his. She had to know she was not dreaming--that he really was a tiger turned into a man.

"Show me again, please?"

Mohan nodded. His warm arms slipped from around her and left her propped up against the bathroom cabinets.

Mohan moved on his hands and knees to the center of the floor, and, sure enough, his body changed shape. It happened much faster this time. Like water, fur slid from his skin, and his head became that of the tiger's. His long tail swished out behind him, and he sat down on his hind legs, waiting and purring loudly as if to try to comfort her.

"How is this possible? How does something like you really exist?"

Trembling, she crawled forward on her own hands and knees. Mo--or rather Mohan-- rubbed against her body. She slid her fingers through his fur.

Her mind was still grappling with what her eyes had seen versus what she believed to be true; that what she had seen was simply impossible.

He shifted back while she was still touching him. She felt the way his hair withdrew. She felt the tremor that ran through his body as he became a man once again.

"You believe now?"

Julia nodded, not knowing what to say to him.

"Good."

Mohan gracefully rose to his feet and crossed the bathroom floor to start the shower. "Come. Varm vater make you feel better," he commented absently. He moved back towards her and crouched down.

Gazing into his face she could see the concern and tenderness in his eyes as he took her hands in his and drew her to her feet.

Still feeling very weak, she offered no protest when Mohan stripped her of her nightgown and set her under the warm spray. Without ceremony, he soaped her down, even washing her hair.

He was right. The warm water was soothing and brought calm to her turbulent thoughts. Her mind was full of questions waiting to burst forth.

She opened her mouth to ask the first one, but he hushed her.

"Vait. I know you have many question. I vill answer all I can. First, let us be settled. Da?"

Julia nodded, not trusting her voice in that moment.

Tugging her out of the shower, he rubbed her down before tending to himself. Julia took the time to clean her teeth before he scooped her into his arms and carried her back into the bedroom.

He settled her under the blankets before returning to the bathroom to retrieve the glass of water. He set it on the nightstand and climbed under the covers, pulling her back flush against his warm skin, wrapping himself around her.

How good it felt to have his skin against hers. Her body knew the man at her back. His breath was warm on her neck; she felt each intake and exhalation of air. It was comforting, soothing. Her mind was overloaded with all the questions bouncing around in her mind.

"How?" was the first she asked.

"How does the vind blow? Moon hang in the sky? Sometimes things just are. I not know the 'how.' Ve are just born this vay."

"That's why you have the stripes on your skin..." Everything about Mohan was starting to fall into place.

"Da. It tells us apart from ordinary humans. Ve are both human and animal. I control my tiger--and his tongue."

With her back pressed against his front, she may not have been able to see Mohan's face, but she still heard the amusement in his tone.

He was teasing her, trying to make her feel at ease. With each passing moment, she was relaxing more and more. Was she starting to accept what Mohan was?

"Everything that happened in your village, and the reason Ashcroft caged you…he knows what you are."

Mohan was silent. "Ve have alvays been hunted, if not for our tiger hides but for being different. Ve tried to stay avay from the vorld, but the vorld grows smaller. Soon ve may not exist. Those he killed vere the last of my kin, my family. I have no vone now."

She twisted around in his arms to face him.

"I'm sorry I accused you of lying last night."

He chuckled, reaching out to brush back a stray hair which had fallen across her face.

"It no matter. You now know truth, and still talking to me. That matter very much."

She gazed into his ice blue depths and realized just how distinctive he truly was. Mohan may defy every known law of nature, but he was a uniquely beautiful creature--and someone she loved no matter what he was.

She also loved Mo and had worried about him since they had left the Snowy Mountain Ranges. It seemed Mohan had been right, Julia mused dryly, that she had not needed to worry about him.

"You're not alone, Mohan. Yes, it was and still is a hell of a shock, but I honestly don't care what you are. I think I would love you no matter what."

After all, he had trusted her enough to show her his most guarded secret. It felt foolish not to at least tell him the secret desire of her heart.

"Vat you love more, tiger or me?" he asked thoughtfully after a moment.

It was Julia's turn to give him an impish grin. "How can I love one without the other?"

The radiant smile that spread across his face made her heart stutter in her chest. He was gorgeous when he smiled, when he frowned…heck, he was still sexy-as-sin.

"Hey, that tiger of yours had to listen to all my ramblings. How could you listen to all that and not tell me! You didn't trust me to tell me sooner?" she accused.

"No ramble. You still have long vind, da. But to me very cute, I like listen to your talking. It sooth me, like soft song. I vorry vhen try to tell you. It is big shock. I think you not love me. You think I be magic, but the real magic is in heart." He captured her hand and pressed it over the left side of his chest. "It takes stronger hearts to leave past behind. Ve may never forget, but ve move forward. Ve live and love against all odds."

How could she not be powerfully moved by Mohan's words? He had gone through hell and back, and all she had to whine about was a lying, unfaithful ex-husband.

She understood, without words, what he was trying to tell her. She blinked back the sudden stinging of tears, which threatened to spill.

"I love you, need you, like plant need vater. I vent to see lavyer. She help me get things vanted of vestern vomen."

She frowned in confusion. "What things?"

He reached across her and retrieved something she hadn't seen from the nightstand. Julia drew in a sharp breath when she saw it was a little black box.

"As tiger and people, ve take mates for lifetime. I vant you for mine. Say da?"

He opened the little black box. The small, inset diamond ring sparkled in the morning sunlight. It was not overly flashy, but elegant and beautiful.

Julia buried her face against his shoulder as she began to sob.

"I no vant to make you cry."

He hugged her tightly to him, running a soothing hand up and down her back.

"I'm sorry," she sniffed. "I'm just so overwhelmed. Yes, of course I'll marry you."

He let out a breath of relief, and she wiped her eyes with the back of her hand.

"Dis good. Those cubs you carry need their father."

She stared at him blankly, not understanding. He chuckled. Removing the ring from its velvet holdings, he took her ring finger and slid it on. The metal was cool against her heated skin, but it quickly warmed and felt comfortable, felt just right.

Mohan shifted slightly and put a gap between their lower bodies. His hand skimmed down to caress her lower stomach. "Vhen in tiger form, ve have stronger senses. Our smell and vision are much stronger. Ve also know things through taste. Vhen I taste you, just before…"

The memory of what she believed to have been a tiger bringing her to orgasm made the heat flush into her cheeks. "I could taste change in your body. You have my cubs in here. You are pregnant."

It took a moment for Mohan's words to skink in. She stared like a stunned mullet.

"I'm pregnant? Are you sure? But how is that possible? I…I thought…"

The grin on his face was one of love and pride. "Da, ve know. Never vrong. Only you vrong in thinking you could not. You no met me."

"Oh, my god. You deliberately set out to get me pregnant?"

"Not first time. After first time, da."

His confession left her head spinning again. She stared at Mohan's sincere expression. He was acting as if it was the most normal thing in the world. She did not know whether to be angry or thrilled at the prospect of being a mother. Mind you, it was something she had secretly always wanted.

So many emotions in such a short time crashed over Julia. Tears slid over the bridge of her nose. She sniffed as the wet drops landed on the pillow.

Even though her vision was blurred, she could see he was worried again. He tugged her closer, cradling her head against his chest. "You no like dis news?"

"No, I mean yes, I mean no… I'm going to be a mum." She cried harder, making his chest wet with her tears. "You've given me something I've always wanted to be."

She felt his chest heave out a breath of relief. "I be vorried you no vant have my cubs."

"Don't ever think that! Yes, I'm a bit miffed in the sneaky way you went about it. Then again, the fault was mine in assuming I couldn't get pregnant." Julia tugged her hand from between their bodies to wipe at her tears. She was so tired. She yawned, and her body relaxed, lying limply in Mohan's arms. She was having trouble thinking straight.

"So much in such a short time, but I honestly couldn't want anything or anyone more than I do you and this baby," she murmured sleepily. "Is there anything else you need to tell me, Mohan?"

"No, I think ve have covered it all. There be no more secrets."

Thank goodness for that. She did not think she could stand anything else in that moment--tiger shifter, a marriage proposal, finding out she was pregnant, all in one hit. Apart from the shifting part, Mohan had given her what she had always longed for; not only to have children, but to have a loving husband and father to her children by her side.

"It be all right. You sleep, *krasIvaya.*" he soothed, tucking her snugly against his side. His warmth was, indeed, soothing. Unable to keep her eyes open any longer, she let sleep claim her.

Chapter Eighteen

"What the hell do you mean I can't go in?" Bill Ashcroft yelled into the phone, after one of his overly paid solicitors delivered him the news he did not want to hear.

His ship had reached the outer waters of New Zealand, and they had been pulled up by the port authorities. They had refused him entry into their waters.

"Mr Ashcroft, I've been monitoring the international activates very carefully. The European Interpol has issued a warrant for your arrest. Someone obviously found out you were illegally hunting in Russia. The charge for illegal poaching I understand, but the charge for first degree murder I don't."

"I don't give a fuck about Russia, Europe or any Interpol charges. They can't touch me. What I want is to get into Australia." Ashcroft's tone turned venomous.

"You are in Australian and New Zealand waters. They do not have a warrant, as you have done nothing wrong on their soil, but they have banned you from entering their area."

Bill's hand shook. He had to physically restrain himself from smashing the phone against the wall in rage.

"I want into Australia! I don't care how you do it, just fucking do it!" he yelled into the phone before slamming it down.

Bill jabbed the intercom button connected to the ship's lounge. "Ivan, get the hell up here."

He sat back, drumming his fingers impatiently on the hard oak tabletop as he waited for his right hand man to arrive.

If there was a way to get things done, Ivan knew the way, no matter where in the world they might be. When Bill had hired him, his accent held traces of so many different places, it was hard to pin down just where he was from. The scars on his face and body told Bill he had road-mapped across the more dangerous parts of the world. Ivan was a mercenary, and he had definitely done things even Bill was fearful of asking about. At any rate, the past did not matter. Bill paid him now, and paid him well enough to make sure things got done.

The door opened, and Ivan stomped loudly into the office, drawing Bill's gaze to the man's ever-present steel-capped boots before skimming up his dark blue and white, military-style uniform. His thick leather belt sported several knives and handguns. Bill knew if you looked beneath the thick jacket or took off Ivan's boots, there would be many more concealed weapons. Ivan was dangerous and deadly.

Ivan shared Bill's taste for hunting and, more so, for killing. Bill paid him well for his wealth of knowledge and expertise.

Ivan was partly to blame for the killing in the Siberian village; his crazed bloodlust had led him to callously shoot and knife every tiger or striped man that had crossed his path.

Ivan folded his arms, making his thick biceps bulge menacingly.

"Do you know anyone who can get us into Australia undetected?"

Ivan's nod was stiff, his gaze cold. "Hunting tiger?"

Bill's slight smile was furtive. "But, of course."

~ * ~

"Will the child be born as a baby or a tiger?"

Mohan gave her a dry look, one she now recognized from Mo. His expressions in tiger form and human were uncannily similar.

"Well, you did say cubs…" She thought about that for a moment. "Oh, cubs. More than one?"

"Da, more than vone. Since I know of no human vho has ever carried our kind before, I vill assume vone or two. And no, they vill be born normal infants. Tiger shifters do not start to shift until around age two."

"Oh..." Well, that was one weight off her mind. "Ever used a litter tray? Do you ever get fur balls?"

She giggled as his stare became one of irritation. She had been peppering her new husband with questions during the long drive back to their Snowy Mountain home. The trailer was again loaded down with supplies Mohan had chosen to help him renovate their old house.

There was no doubt they would go back to live there. Julia felt even more connected to her grandfather's old house now they were turning it into a family home. It was where she had met Mohan and found the love of her life. It was also a place far from the thrum of the world--where they could raise their children away from prying eyes.

Raewin had pushed through the usual one-month waiting period for marriage licenses, but they still had to wait two weeks before they could be married.

As soon as the word was out Julia was engaged, her friends had swamped her to get a chance to ogle her new man. They had taken over her house, rushing to organize a thrown-together wedding. Julia had been planning on just a quiet civil ceremony at the Melbourne Register's office.

Her friends from the clothing store--where she used to work before her divorce--had ushered her out of the house to have her pampered and primed. Her friends' husbands had taken Mohan on an Aussie pub crawl, declaring it was the only way to end your life as a single man.

Julia smiled at the memory of him alighting from the driver's seat of her Rover later that evening, while his new drunken friends all stumbled out of the back, declaring what a great guy Mohan was.

The wedding had taken place in the parlour of her house with at least ten guests in attendance. Julia had tried to invite her mother, but she only got a nasty reply on her answering machine.

It seemed marrying Mohan was the proverbial final straw in her mother's hat, and she had declared Julia disowned. As wedding gifts went, it was the best one her mother could have given her.

Julia relaxed in the passenger seat and enjoyed the ride home, not bothered in the slightest that Mohan wanted to drive. She fiddled with the new ring on her finger and smiled, watching the sunlight reflect off Mohan's plain gold band.

She had a husband she adored and a child or two growing within her. Life could not get any better.

For the first time in her life, she did not feel like she was wasting it, feeling instead this was how it was meant to be; richly-lived with those you love surrounding you. In Mohan's sense of the word, life was purrrfect.

Her mind was still overactive with questions about Mohan. She wanted to know every little detail about shifter life.

"Did you…um...have you ever...well, you know?"

He raised an eyebrow in curiosity, probably taking good note of how deeply she blushed. It was bad enough coming to terms with the fact he enjoyed licking her in tiger form--and the fact she liked it too.

"You cute vhen ask sex question." Mohan chuckled. Damn. Well, she guessed it was not that hard to tell. "Go, ask."

"Did you ever have sex while you had shifted and...well, your partner had not?"

Mohan's smile was utterly roguish. "Vant to try?"

Julia just stared at him with her mouth open. His laugh was full and deep. "Ve no have sex while shifted. My cock changes to cat form, and it also has barb on end. It painful when the male pulls from the voman also vhile in tiger form. I also have claws. They vould scratch a back to ribbons. It no good, unless you be a tiger also. I vould never do that to you. Sex always much better as man than tiger." He winked at her.

Julia let out a breath of relief.

"But I know you like my tongue. My voman taste sweet like honey." Now he was teasing her.

She gave him a playful shove. "Next, you'll be telling me you eat tiger chow."

"Da, it very tasty." He never even batted an eyelash.

Julia wrinkled her nose in disgust. "Ewww! Now I think about, all that raw meat you ate..."

"Vas very good meat. I know some people like rare steak," he defended with a half smile.

Julia gave a huff. "Well, if you don't behave yourself, I know where you'll be having your meals from now on."

He chuckled. "You act like old married voman already."

Julia bit her lip to stop her retort. Instead, she shifted in her seat and moved closer. She slid her hand up along her husband's thigh, and the back of her hand brushed against his obviously hard cock. "Oh, but would an old married woman do this for her husband?"

"Julia, I be driving," Mohan warned softly. His tone had dropped an octave and was husky, laced with desire as she eased down his zipper.

Knowing Mohan was a commando guy to the core, it didn't take much for her to set free his ridged length.

"Then drive. Keep your hands on the wheel, your eyes on the road, and leave everything else to me," she murmured, her mouth actually watering at the thought of tasting his cock.

It was deliciously long and wide enough for her to just wrap her fingers around it. She shuddered in arousal at how good it felt thrusting within her. His length was richly veined. The head of his cock had a dark purple, weeping mushroom head. It looked angry and painful. She inhaled his aroused, musky male scent, something she loved to smell. Just like a cat, she wanted to rub it all over her.

Mohan shifted his hips lower. She inwardly chuckled, knowing he wanted this despite his earlier warning. She glanced up to see his knuckles white on the steering wheel, his gaze fixed on the road.

"Oh, my poor kitty. Want me to kiss this better."

Mohan's low growl sent her own desire onto overdrive. She felt him tense up as she reached in, circling her hand around his base and protecting it from the fabric and metal zipper of his jeans. Her head was between his arms and the steering wheel. She flicked her tongue over his weeping head.

His sharp intake of breath and long low growl spurred her on. She circled his cock head with her tongue before sucking it into her mouth. Softly, she applied a suctioning pressure as she continued to taste his salty, slightly bitter flavour.

Stroking him at the base of his cock, she moved her mouth up and down, taking him as deep as she could. Low moans escaped her own throat as she sucked harder.

She felt one of his hands settle on the top of her head. He thrust his hip up towards her mouth to urge her on, faster. She responded in kind, breathing in through her nose and sucking him harder, pumping him with her fist.

The sudden pressure of the seatbelt around her waist and Mohan's hand on her head stopped her from flying forward as the car screeched to a sudden stop.

The engine of the Rover vibrated as he jerked on the hand brake. Both hands were now on her, one stroking her back while the other still cradled her head. His hips jerked higher. Beneath the palm of her hand she felt his body tremble. She slid her tongue down the side of his cock feeling his veins throb and pulse. She knew what was coming. She took him deep down the back of her throat as his cry tore through the interior of the car. A gush of fluids spilled down her throat.

Julia swallowed quickly before having to pull back to take a deep breath. She pulled away and glanced up. Her heart shone with pride seeing the expression of rapture on his handsome face.

Slowly his eyes opened, and he turned his head towards her. His expression was one of awe and love. "Voman, I no can drive if you do that to me." He clicked open her seatbelt to drag her across and onto his lap. His thumb wiped away a dribble of semen which had escaped her mouth.

She licked his finger and grinned at him. "I guess it's true any species of male can't concentrate on two things at the same time," she teased.

"Damn voman. I thought I no love you more than I do now. Clearly I be vrong," Mohan murmured, brushing his lips softly across hers before he pulled her tighter and increased the pressure. He took her mouth in a hungry, passionate kiss. She melted into him, so strong and so sure around her. She kissed him back with all the love she felt bursting within. When he pulled back, she felt dizzy and breathless.

"We'd better keep going if we're going to reach home before dark," she managed to whisper.

"Da. Beautiful vife know I vill finish this vhen ve get home," he promised.

As she settled back into her seat, she had no doubt he would.

Chapter Nineteen

Due to Mohan's failure at keeping his hands off his curvaceous, sexy wife, they had arrived home later than expected the previous night. He had stopped at least twice to fuck her. First was on the back seat; the second time, he playfully chased her into the surrounding bushland while in his tiger form. Then he shifted and took her from behind, up against the smooth-barked trunk of a native gum tree. By the time they had arrived home, it was late.

They had bought takeout food to eat in the car, so as soon as they reached the house, he had picked her up in his arms and carried her inside. They made love on the bed until they were both too exhausted to move.

Now it was early morning. Mohan softly kissed his wife's forehead, content he was leaving her sleeping soundly. Considering how many times he had made her come yesterday, and considering her pregnant state, he was sure she would sleep for a few hours yet.

Julia murmured something unintelligible before turning over and snuggling deeper under the thick quilt cover. He smiled and walked silently from the room. He sat down in one of the camp chairs and pulled on his treasured Warragul work boots. He picked up the keys to her car and, just as quietly, left the house and locked the door behind him.

The sun was just starting to rise, and a thin layer of snow lay about the ground and over the house. He breathed in the rich, clean, cool mountain air. The smells of the native fauna were a *welcome home* to his senses. He climbed in the rover and started the engine. Easily, he navigated the long dirt road off Julia's property and onto the main road. He had a few errands to run in town, including supplies to pick up in order to make some more furniture.

Julia and her smart mind had suggested he might turn his skill at carpentry into a profitable business. Rich, arty-type people in the city would apparently pay big dollars for the type of table he had made for her from the native wood. He enjoyed working with his hands, and he needed something to supply an income. The money the Russian government had given him would not last forever. He knew she had money, but it was his responsibility to care for her, in every regard. He did not want to rely on her wealth--it was a matter of pride.

Second on his list was to visit a certain real estate agent who needed to be put in his place especially when it came to his wife.

The township was still sleepy. The supply store was just opening for early trade. Mohan parked in front and stepped out to observe the few cars which ambled by; store owners starting unlocking their front doors.

Outside of the car, Mohan was assaulted by the mouth-watering scents of freshly baked products from the town's local bakery. It gave him a mind to take something back for Julia.

As he was about to enter the hardware store, he spotted his target. John Leeman was trudging across the asphalt with a steaming cup and a large paper bag of baked goods in his pudgy hands. Mohan watched as the man fumbled with the key to his office while trying to hold on to what was obviously his breakfast. Finally, he managed to get the door unlocked and stumbled inside.

Mohan strode purposefully across the short distance to the real estate office. The bell above the door rang loudly as he shoved it open and walked inside. John Leeman, clearly startled, glanced up from his desk. His eyes narrowed in distaste as Mohan approached. Leeman set down his food and turned to face him.

"I would have thought the immigration department would have picked you up by now," he sneered.

Mohan carefully chose his English words. "No law can touch me. I am legal. Julia is my voman, and if you ever threaten her, or even look at her in a manner she or I do not like..."

Mohan grabbed the small, beady-eyed man by his white shirt and shoved him back roughly against the wall, pinning him there. Respectable fear now entered into Leeman's expression as he struggled uselessly against Mohan's strength.

"The pieces of you left will not be identifiable," Mohan finished in a low growl.

Leeman swallowed and nodded. Mohan released him and stepped back. He was through dealing with weasels like this. He turned his back, satisfied he had scared the man into staying away from his wife.

"You'll get yours yet," Leeman said shakily from behind him. "In fact, those you've been hiding from will hang your freakish hide out to dry."

Mohan frowned, trying to make sense of Leeman's words. The pit of his stomach dropped as he knew the only person he had been hiding from was Bill Ashcroft. Anger curled through Mohan, and, in the next moment, he launched himself at Leeman and slammed him against the wall. This time his hand was curled around Leeman's throat as he lifted the agent a foot off the floor. Leeman clawed at Mohan's hand, struggling to get breath into his lungs.

"Tell me vhat you have done little man, or I kill you right now." He stared into Leeman's dark eyes. Mohan loosened his hold just enough to allow him to rasp out his words.

"A rich American and some other men came last night. Paid me well to tell them where you were."

Julia. He had left her alone in the house. The sudden fear of losing Julia heightened his anger. Mohan wanted nothing more than to snap the weasel's neck. Instead, he yanked back his hand and slugged him hard in the face. Leeman's eyes rolled back into his head, and he crumpled to the floor in a bloodied heap. Mohan ignored the throbbing of his hand and raced to the door. He ripped it open and sprinted to the car, jumping into the driver's seat. He fumbled with the car keys but managed to ring the keyhole and shove the key into the ignition, praying to god as he did he would reach his Julia before they did. The tires squealed as he shoved the car into gear and planted his foot on the gas pedal.

~ * ~

Kookaburras were laughing. Julia groaned, wishing she could put a timer on the darned birds to wake her up at a later time. She yawned and stretched before fumbling for her watch. She had left it on the makeshift side table that consisted of a cardboard packing box. It was just after nine--not too early, but not too late either. Her head felt groggy. Her body was still tired. Then she smiled, knowing Mohan was the reason for it all. She gave her naked belly a rub.

"Hello, my boys." It was a mother's instinct to know the sex of her unborn babies, she thought. Julia was not worried in the slightest Mohan was not still in bed with her. She knew he would be up and hard at work already. She threw off the covers, and instantly the chilled air made her skin prickle with goose bumps. She snatched her satin robe from the end of the bed and wrapped it around her. She ignored her cold feet as she stepped onto the bare floor. They had not yet unpacked the trailer, which included several floor rugs. The sound of heavy boots thudding though the house, followed by a metal clanging, made her smile again. She opened the door and walked down the hall to find out what her new husband was up to in the kitchen.

"That had better be scrambled eggs you're making so much noise over, tiger boy."

She rounded the corner into the open living area. Julia stopped dead, instantly sobered as four pairs of male eyes stared at her.

"Tiger boy. I assume that would be Mohan," asked a tall bulky man with an American accent. He was dressed in military camouflage, as was the hard-looking wiry man on his right. The other two, dressed in jeans and common flannelette shirts, hung in the background. What she certainly did not miss were the huge rifles hanging from their hands or slung over their shoulders.

"Who the hell are you?!" she demanded as fear stole though her. "Where is my husband?"

The American raised an eyebrow, turning to the man on his right.

"It seems the tiger has taken a mate." His eyes swept over her from head to toe, making her want to shudder in disgust. It suddenly occurred to Julia this must be Bill Ashcroft. But how had he found his way into the country? Then again, if Mohan was able to get in undetected, a man with a heck of a lot of money could too. Julia swallowed. She was in a lot of trouble. She backed up a foot before spinning on her heel and bolting.

"Grab her! If our tiger has taken her as a mate, she will be useful to use as bait."

A scream tore from her throat, as she was slammed hard against the back door before she could reach for the handle. The impact knocked the breath from her lungs, yet it did not stop her from fighting like a wildcat when two of the men caught her upper arms and dragged her back towards the living area. Julia reeled with the pain that exploded across her face as one of them slapped her after she had bit his hand and kicked the other in the groin. They shoved her into a camp chair. She cradled her hurt face and, using her other arm, protectively covered her stomach. If any of them hit her there, she could lose the babies.

"You know he's going to rip all your throats out." Julia kept her tone calm and, she hoped, menacing.

Ashcroft had cold grey eyes. His thinning dark hair was peppered with grey, and his face was wrinkled and weather-beaten. He crouched down before her.

"You see, a creature like Mohan, he's neither man nor beast. He falls into a complete category of his own. This makes him very unique and very collectable. Don't worry. I don't want to kill him; I just want to add him to my collection. I am curious, though. Did he fuck you in tiger form or just in human form?"

Incensed by the rudeness of Ashcroft, Julia slapped him across the face before she could stop herself. Ashcroft rose to tower over her, rubbing the side of his face.

"All right, little kitten. Maybe I'll keep you alive just to watch him fuck you in tiger form." He glanced down to her stomach, and, by the critical manner with which he was sizing her up, a cold sweat of fear broke over her body. The thought of him finding out she was pregnant by Mohan made her feel ill.

"I wonder if he can get you pregnant." Ashcroft's tone was thoughtful. "Or has he already?"

Julia pursed her lips. She was not going to give up that information easily--but it did not matter.

He knew just how to get his answer. Ashcroft stepped back and said, "Ivan, hit her in the stomach."

"Nooo!" screamed Julia, as the thin wiry man moved towards her with his hand curled into a fist.

His cold expression never wavered. Julia put both hands across her belly.

"Please, don't. I…I am pregnant." Tears stung the back of her eyes. They escaped, spilling down her cheeks.

A smile of triumph crossed Ashcroft's face. "It seems we may not have to capture our tiger after all. We have a new, precious cargo to take care of. Prepare for a full hunt, boys. I want a white tiger head, first in my bag and mounted on my wall back in the states before this week's through."

Julia's jaw dropped. Good god, she had no idea men like Bill Ashcroft actually existed in the world. He was the essence of pure evil. She now had a full understanding of the horrors Mohan had been through. This less-than-human man with no soul or conscious had destroyed everything of Mohan's. Now Ashcroft was planning to take his life--and take away the babies she carried.

"Are you going to behave, little mother? You wouldn't want your precious cargo to be hurt now." Julia narrowed her eyes on Ashcroft. She knew if he wanted a chance at having tiger-shifter cubs, then he would not want them hurt either. There was no way in hell she was going to help them get to Mohan.

"Go to hell," she spat.

"Very well. Ivan, assist our bait to the capture sight. You make her lose the cubs, and you'll have me to deal with."

The one called Ivan did not look impressed by Ashcroft's threat as he stepped forward. Then Julia made the mistake of glaring up at the man. Her eyes widened in sudden fear as the man threw back his shoulder. Julia did not have time to scream before he punched her in the face, knocking her clean out.

~ * ~

The Rover skidded to a halt. Mohan bolted out of the vehicle and bounded up the steps. The door was wide open; fear of what he would find made his heart pound. Carefully, he peered into their home. Instantly, he knew Julia was not there. The turned over chair and spots of blood on the living room floor had Mohan's blood running cold in fear. He was too late. He knew they had her.

Quickly, he stripped off his clothing and shifted. He began sniffing around the area, and from the distinct odours he could tell there were four males. Julia's sweet smell was mixed with the powerful scent of her freshly spilled blood. Knowing they had hurt her, he was going to gut them with his claws from throat to navel and listen to them scream. He followed the trail of Julia's blood out of the house and across the grass to the line of trees leading into the forest. It was obvious they were using Julia as bait. He drew small comfort from the fact they would keep her alive in order to trap him. Mohan knew he had to tread with care. His life did not matter so much as the lives of the woman he loved and his cubs growing within her.

Singling out the scent of one of the men, he saw it headed off in a different direction from where Julia had been dragged. They had taken everything from him once, but not again. Mohan flattened his ears and flicked his tail. Crouching down and using every sense he had, he went into full stalking mode. It was time to hunt--and kill--his prey.

Chapter Twenty

Julia woke in a haze of pain. Her entire head throbbed. She wanted to cradle her face and curl up into the fetal position and whimper. She wanted Mohan's comforting arms around her. Instead, she could not move her wrists. They were tied securely above her head. When she tugged at them, the rough rope bit painfully into her tender flesh.

Opening her eyes made her wince. The side of her face was painfully swollen. She glanced down. At least she still had on her robe, which did little to protect her against the chill of the high mountain air. Her feet and limbs were numb with cold. She was tied to a narrow, rough-barked tree, almost dead center of the clearing. She glanced around the surrounding forest. She could not hear nor see anyone. For certain, she felt like the worm on the hook. And Mohan was the big fish they wanted to catch. No doubt they were lying in wait for him to come charging in to her rescue. Surely these men could not be that dumb? Mohan was a hell of a lot smarter than to come barging into a well-set trap. She would skin his hide herself if he did fall for it. She struggled harder, twisting her wrists, trying to loosen them. She bit down on her lower lip to stop, whimpering from the pain. She only managed to hurt her wrists even more, possibly cutting off the circulation. Not that there was much blood getting to them as it was, seeing as they were tied above her head.

Everything in the forest went silent. The birds and even the gentle, cool wind seemed to still. The only sound Julia could hear was the pounding of her heart against her ribcage. She hitched her breath to listen. Suddenly, she jumped. A loud shot had rung out, scattering birds. It was followed by a short, strangled scream. Then all fell silent again as if it had never happened. Julia's breathing became short and choppy as the panic rose. If she did not calm down, she was going to hyperventilate and pass out. As much as she wanted the bliss of blackness, she forced her brain into gear and ordered herself to take deep, slow breaths. She had her babies to think about, and she had to be aware of what was happening.

From a different direction, she clearly heard Mohan's tiger snarling. Then more shots rang out, and there was a yell before it again fell silent. How many seconds or minutes went by, she had no idea. They seemed to drag. A crackle of leaves made her turn her head towards the sound; a snapping branch in the opposite direction, and she turned her head quickly the other way, hoping to catch a glimpse of something, anything. And that was when all hell broke loose.

Ashcroft came stumbling wildly out of the bush. Deep scratches bleeding from his arm told her Mohan had attacked him. A long, wickedly sharp-looking knife was gripped in his hand as he headed straight for her. Her eyes widened. She cringed in sudden fear. He was going to kill her. But instead, he swung the blade and sliced right through the ropes that bound her. Like rocks, her arms dropped to her sides, but she was given no respite. The blood rushing back into her limbs made them throb. Then burning pain exploded across her scalp. Julia screamed as Ashcroft grabbed her by her hair and pulled her to her feet.

"Hurry up, bitch. If you make one wrong move, I will gut you, babies or not." His panicked voice was laboured, breathless in her ear. Hooking his hand around her arm, he started pushing her through the bushland ahead of him. From behind came the sound of snarling and grunting, growing louder with each step they took. Branches breaking made them both turn their heads.

Locked in mortal combat were Ivan and tiger Mohan. Even though Ivan was putting up a hell of a fight, Mohan's tiger bulk, his weight and his strength, were no match for the smaller man. Ivan broke free, rolling over before jumping into a crouch. Ivan's clothes had been slashed, and his chest was covered in blood. There was blood on Mohan's paws and around his mouth. Ivan reached to his boot, pulling out a concealed knife.

"Come, you overgrown house cat," goaded Ivan.

She watched transfixed as Mohan crouched low, his ears flattened back just as an angry house cat would do. His eyes locked on Ivan and the deadly knife grasped in his fist.

Julia wanted to scream at him not to do it or he would be killed. She bit her tongue, trusting Mohan knew what he was doing. Like watching a horror movie in slow motion, Mohan leapt--but in midflight, he shifted, breaking Ivan's concentration. Mohan knocked back Ivan's hand, and the knife flew out of reach. At the same moment, Mohan landed a punch squarely into Ivan's bloodied chest. Then he shifted again before Ivan could shake off the punch.

Julia felt the blood drain from her face as she watched Mohan pounce and snarl. His jaws and sharp teeth sank into Ivan's throat and neck. The sickening sound of breaking bones was not something she had ever heard before, but she knew instinctively what it was--a sound she was likely to never forget. Ivan's bloody body dropped from Mohan's jaws.

Julia could only stare in horrified shock as he turned his cold blue eyes towards them. She could see his gaze flicker over her then move past her to Ashcroft. His intent was clear: He was going to kill the man.

Ashcroft knew it too. He pulled her tightly back against his body to shield himself from Mohan. Julia was not sure who shook more, Ashcroft or herself. She felt the coolness of a blade pressed against her throat and knew Ashcroft held his knife there.

"Stay where you are," Ashcroft yelled, almost sending her deaf in her left ear. "I swear I will kill her."

Mohan shifted, his bloodied fur receding. The blood that had stained his pelt now covered his skin. Julia could see several other cuts and wounds along his body. He met her frightened gaze.

"Don't vorry, *krasIvaya.* You trust me, da?"

Julia would have nodded if the blade was not so tightly pressed against her throat. She drew in a breath. Her "yes" was barely audible, even in her own ears. That was the whole point. She did trust him, even if she had just seen him kill a man. But she would do the same thing in order to protect those she cared most about. Mohan and the babies were her life.

"Shut up, both of you!" Ashcroft demanded. "You stay where you are if you want the woman to live." He stumbled back a step back, dragging her along with him.

Mohan remained still as Ashcroft slowly dragged her away. She understood Mohan was not willing to risk her life. Julia calmed her mind enough to try and think rationally. She knew little about self-defense and now wished she had learned. Step after step, they moved far enough away from Mohan to give Ashcroft enough confidence to lower the knife, grip her bicep, and make a run for it.

It was then Julia saw her chance. She pretended to trip on a branch, falling face-first into the leafy, moss-covered ground. She hid the fact she had just picked up a thick dry branch.

"Get up, you stupid bitch," he went for her hair again, yanking it painfully. Curling her fingers around the hard branch she gripped it tightly to stop them from trembling. With her feet planted she rose up, and jabbed the piece of wood as hard as she could straight into his groin.

He let go of her hair as he crouched down to protectively cover his dick. She quickly stood up over him. A loud *thwack* echoed through the forest as she brought the branch down on to his head. The force of it made Julia stumble backwards and fall heavily on her arse. Not once did she hear Mohan following them, but his white and black stripes suddenly blurred before her as he leapt onto Bill Ashcroft, snarling and clawing at the man.

Julia turned and crawled away from both of them. She gripped a thin tree and pulled herself to her feet. Bill Ashcroft lay in a bleeding heap, but he was still breathing as Mohan backed up and shifted once again.

"Please," begged Ashcroft.

Mohan stood over him, holding the knife Ashcroft had used on Julia.

"Vhy should I spare you? Did you spare my family? Any of the children?" growled Mohan.

~ * ~

Mohan froze at the sound of Julia's distraught sob. He turned his head to glance at her. The look of utter distress on her bruised and battered face lifted the red haze of pure hatred and revenge from his eyes. His hand, trembling, still gripped the knife, but he hesitated in sinking the blade into Ashcroft's chest. The man deserved to die. He had killed everything Mohan had ever known. Why should he let the man who ripped him from his world and threatened his new family live?

"Mohan?"

Her soft, trembling voice sent another wave of doubt through his mind.

"Please, hasn't there been enough death? Enough killing?"

He glanced down at the cause of so much pain, but all he felt was pity. The man was worthless, useless. Mohan knew in that moment what was more important to him, Julia and the babies. She had already seen him kill a man in tiger form. If he killed Ashcroft now, it would be in cold blood. The last thing he wanted was Julia looking at him with fear in her eyes. They had both suffered enough.

He tossed the blade a far distance, curled his fist and pounded it solidly into Ashcroft's face until he was satisfied the man would not be waking up for some time to come. He rose as Julia was struggling to climb to her feet. He quickly caught her by the arms. The soft dark red of her satin robe was askew, revealing the soft paleness of her skin, along with the scrapes and bruises. His wounds hurt like hell, but he pushed it all aside to bend down and place his arm under her knees. He lifted her securely against his chest. Tears streamed down her cheeks.

"I was so scared for you and the babies," she sobbed. Her tears were wet and warm on his naked skin.

He carried her back towards the house, knowing he would still have to tend to the mess of hunters.

"It vill be all right, *krasIvaya*," he soothed. "I be all right. I take you to hospital. Check babies."

"I love you. I'm so sorry, I--"

"Hush, voman. I love you too. Trust me to take care of things, da."

Her wet eyelashes closed before she and Mohan reached the Rover, and she was asleep in his arms. He settled her into the car before grabbing a change of clothes, as well as Julia's handbag with her cell phone--he had a few calls to make on the drive to the hospital.

Chapter Twenty-one

It tore at his heart every time she tossed in her sleep and screamed. He would hold her tightly in his arms until she settled again. He snarled at the medical staff when they tried to ask him to leave. They soon realized he was the only thing which could soothe her. The only other person standing a close vigil was Raewin.

After he had contacted the Russian embassy and the local police, he had called her and explained that somehow Bill Ashcroft had gained entry into Australia and had almost killed both of them.

Within a few hours, Raewin had barreled in to take charge of the situation. She talked to the police, who were constantly asking questions, and to the Russian Agents who had found Ashcroft and taken him into their custody. When wildlife experts turned up asking about the animal that had killed the other men, Mohan had claimed ignorance. Park rangers asked if they could set up traps on Julia's land, for they were certain it was a tiger they were trying to catch. They could set traps all they wanted. He did not care about any of it--the only thing that consumed his thoughts was why Julia would not wake up. What was wrong with her? What could he do for her? He felt utterly helpless.

By the third day, he had cornered the small town doctor to demand he do something to wake her up.

"There is nothing physically wrong with your wife. Your twins are healthy and strong. But sometimes the body and the mind need time to heal themselves after such a trauma. Give her time. She will wake," the doctor assured him.

Raewin placed a hand on his shoulder.

"She'll be okay. Julia is a tough woman and has a hell of a lot to live for." Raewin offered her own form of comfort. "The police have finished poking around, and the park will monitor the area for the animal that killed the other men. I have to head back to the city soon."

Mohan glanced at the lawyer, grateful for her help. "Thank you. What about John Leeman?"

"It seems he's run. There is no sign of him anywhere."

The shrill sound of Raewin's cell phone ringing made her turn her back. She snapped the phone from her pocket and strode a few feet out of the hospital room, but she stayed within earshot of Mohan.

"Really? When did this happen?"

Mohan, still holding Julia's hand, raised his head to see Raewin, with a triumphant smile on her face, sidle back into the room.

"It seems some fates just can't be avoided. Our friend Bill Ashcroft suffered a major heart attack while trying to bribe the Russian agents into letting him go. Needless to say, the man will never bother you again."

Mohan stared at the lawyer in surprise. The news of Ashcroft's death was not unwelcome. It meant he and Julia could truly live in peace. It was a huge weight off both their shoulders, but he still worried about why she would not wake up.

Raewin glanced at Julia's face. The bruises, although healing, still stood out against the paleness of her skin. She shook her head.

"Are you going to be okay?"

"Yes, ve vill be fine," he assured her.

Raewin sighed. "I would stay longer if I could..." She hesitated.

"No, your assistance has been invaluable. I know, if she could, Julia would thank you for all you have done."

Raewin nodded. "Remember, call me if you have any more issues with the police. I should have the rest of this wrapped up soon. I am confident the deaths will stay out of the courts, as it was clearly an animal who killed those men. Very strange, but still…you know where to get me."

Mohan gave a curt nod but remained silent. He could almost see Raewin's mind at work. With nothing more to say, she gathered her briefcase from where it sat by the door and glided out of the hospital room. Mohan turned his full attention back to Julia. He stroked the back of her hand and talked to her in Russian about the things he wanted to do in their house. He talked himself hoarse until he fell asleep across the side of her bed.

~ * ~

Julia wondered why she could not move her hand. It was a little sweaty and weighted down with something heavy. She tugged at it, trying to free it from the weight. Her eyelids felt like they were glued together, and her body ached like she had not moved her muscles in a long time. Prying her eyes open, she had to blink several times to clear up her blurred vision.

The first thing that came into focus was a little florescent light overhead against a white patterned ceiling consisting of little crisscrossed silver lines. She blinked again and licked her dry, parched lips. She needed some water. Glancing down the length of the bed, she saw the reason why she could not move her hand. Mohan's dark head lay across it. His hand encased hers. Never before had she had the chance to see her gorgeous Siberian husband asleep. She had always fallen asleep before he had, and he was always awake before she was. His usually tense features were relaxed, at peace. It made him appear more youthful; the dark shadow of his facial hair giving him an exotically handsome look. When he smiled at her, he always set her heart aflutter and her body aflame. Julia was filled with pride this distinctive man was all hers.

The urge to touch him almost outweighed her need for water. She tugged at her hand again, causing him to stir. His eyebrow twitched, and his expression changed as his eyes opened. His first expression was one of sleepy confusion. It was so cute, and Julia smiled down at him. Staring into his beautiful blue depths, she watched the sleep slip from his gaze, and his expression change to one of awareness.

He raised his head, blinking as he stared at her.

"You be vake?"

Managing to pull her tingling hand free, she pointed it to the jug of water and two upside down cups on the side table.

"Please," she croaked.

Mohan knew what she wanted.

He stumbled to his feet, and she watched as his trembling hands snatched the glass and almost spilled the water as he hastily poured it. Julia's arms felt weak as she struggled to sit up, but Mohan hooked his arm around her shoulders and helped her forward. Then he pressed the glass against her lips. The cool water ran down her dry, sore throat, soothing it. She took several long gulps.

"Thank you." She took in a deep breath.

Mohan set the glass back on the side table and helped her lie back down. Worry mixed with relief shown on his face.

"How you feeling?" he asked. His expression made her feel anxious.

"I feel good, why? What's wrong?" she could not help asking. Her mind went back over what had happened before she had passed out in Mohan's arms: Ashcroft, the men, the pain. But none of that worried her any longer. Perhaps there was something else that had happened she did not know about, something he was not telling her. Her mind flew to her babies. She glanced down at her stomach, placing her hand over it.

"Are the babies...?" she swallowed in sudden fear.

"No, Julia. Babies are fine. Doctor say so. I be so vorried, you no wake up for many days. I no can lose you!" His voice cracked with emotion as he suddenly pulled her into his arms, almost smothering her.

"Oh, sweetheart! It's okay." Her voice was muffled against his chest. "How long have I been out?" She wrapped her arms around him.

"Three days."

Julia drew in a deep breath. "What happened with Ashcroft? Did the police come?"

Mohan released her from his grasp and cradled her more gently against him while he explained how Raewin had come to help deal with the stream of police and other authorities. Then he informed her Ashcroft was dead of a heart attack.

Well, there was Karma for you, she thought. Despite everything she had been through, she did not feel that bad. Hearing Ashcroft was dead--and not by Mohan's hand or jaws--brought a sense of relief.

"He'll certainly rot in hell then," she concluded after a long moment in silence.

Mohan shook his head. "I no understand how you sound so calm. I vorry. After all you've seen, the vay they hurt you, you have many bad dreams vhile sleeping."

She did not doubt Mohan's words. She did remember bad dreams, but they were nothing but a distant memory in her mind. It was probably for the best. As for sleeping so long, her body obviously had needed the rest, and, knowing Mohan, he would not have left her side.

"Hey, so I slept like Sleeping Beauty for a few days, but I have my handsome prince to kiss me and wake me up from the nightmares. If there is one thing I have learned from all of this, it is I am pretty damn sure I can face anything as long as I have you."

The look of utter love on his face made her want to cry.

"Da, you have me, my heart, my soul, alvays."

Julia adored this man. She did not want to cry; yet she needed a more intimate comfort.

"Then stop worrying, and kiss me already."

He did so, softly, gently and frustratingly slowly, as if he was frightened of hurting her.

Julia wanted to feel his arms around her and the heated passion she knew was her man. When she tugged on the back of his neck, running her tongue along his, he very quickly got the message. And he kissed her just how she loved him to kiss her, leaving her breathless, dizzy, and always wanting more.

"Ahem…" Someone cleared their throat from the doorway.

Mohan broke the kiss and pulled back, turning his attention to the hospital nurse who was waiting--and looking rather sheepish.

"Mr *Alexandrov,* you were supposed to inform the nursing staff when your wife woke up." Sonya was the name on her ID badge. The solidly built middle-aged woman bustled into the room and began checking all of Julia's vitals. She removed the IV from her arm.

Mohan hovered like a hawk, making the nurse snap at him several times to move out of her way. The nurse finally stopped and wrote everything down on the chart at the foot of the bed.

"Um, I'm feeling fine. A bit stiff, and most definitely could use a shower, but I want to go home." Julia felt just how weak she was when she tried to sit up again. The nurse, helped by Mohan, propped her up against the pillows. Julia was miffed when Nurse Sonya turned her stern gaze to Mohan and addressed him instead of her.

"She's not to leave until the doctor has seen her in the morning. You can help her in the shower if you want, but she's also carrying twins and needs extra care."

"I vill take very good care of my vife," Mohan said indignantly.

Julia struggled to suppress a grin.

"Right. I'll go get some food from the kitchen. You need to regain your strength. Until then, you stay put."

Both Julia and Mohan nodded.

Nurse Sonya seemed satisfied she had made her point and left the two of them alone.

Julia grinned at Mohan. "Now, about that shower…"

His smile was infectious. He ripped off her bed sheets and lifted her into his arms. It felt so good go be held in his strong arms as he carried her into the bathroom. With her arms wrapped around the one man she loved more than life itself, she knew from this point on, life could only get better.

Epilogue

Julia loved the freshly carved scent of wood shavings mixed with vanish and timber polish. The humming of the engine and the deep rumble of the lathe greeted her as she pushed open the door and closed it quietly behind her. She stood for several moments, just watching Mohan at work. There was a look of utter concentration on his face as he gripped the carving tool in his hand. His muscles bunched as he pressed it into the fast spinning piece of timber. Timber bits flew in all directions as the piece started to take shape under his careful positioning.

He pulled back and nodded to himself, seemingly satisfied with his work, before reaching out to switch off the lathe. It slowed to a stop, leaving a beautiful, long, carved piece of wood.

She was confronted with a sudden jealousy over the piece of wood as Mohan lovingly caressed his handiwork.

"Should I leave you two alone?" she teased lightly.

Mohan turned his head, giving her a heart-thumping grin. Even after all this time, all he had to do was smile at her, and she melted like butter. He ripped off his glasses and dusted off his shirt.

"Vill be good piece," he murmured thoughtfully, glancing back at the carved wood one more time before giving her his full attention.

Julia moved around his central workbench to show him the paper she held in her hand. Mohan took the paper, ignoring it and setting it on the bench. He pulled her into his arms and captured her mouth in a leisurely kiss. It quickly deepened into something hungrier, more carnal.

He ended the kiss and pulled back to ask huskily, "Vhere are boys?"

"Hmm. I put them down for a nap about five minutes ago." Julia was not going let her husband get away with kissing her like that then stop. She slid her hand down to his jeans, cupping him through the material. "I say we have a good twenty minutes before they wake up, tiger boy."

"Good, I be hungry." He pulled back. "Strip, voman."

She did not need to be asked twice. Giggling, Julia began working at the buttons of her top, tugging it off, followed by her bra. Mohan had already pulled off his shirt and shoved down his jeans. He was already naked while she still struggled with her pants. She never bothered with underwear anymore, as Mohan tended to shred them to pieces and would then casually ask why she needed them in the first place.

Julia gave a squeal as Mohan scooped her up and carried her to an old sofa he had recently picked up at the local second hand dealer's store. He tossed her onto it and finished pulling down her pants, flinging them onto the floor. He always had been more proficient at getting her naked than she had been. He pounced on her, hungrily devouring her mouth. Julia writhed against him, loving the friction of her breasts pressed against his hard chest.

Her head spun when he left her mouth and placed open-mouthed kisses along the side of her jaw and over her neck. Julia ran her fingers over his shoulders and back. She could never get enough of touching her husband in every way. She let out a soft moan when Mohan sucked on the sensitive spot between her neck and shoulder. His hands plumped her breasts, and he skipped his tongue down to lovingly flick it over each nipple. He purred as he sucked one into his mouth, his fingers now skimming a path down between the junction of her thighs. She widened them to let him play as he wished. He found her clit easily as he switched breasts.

Julia threw her head back, basking in the heated pleasure he was wringing from her. She gasped when he pulled back. His firm strong hands gripped her hips and flipped her onto her stomach. Her knees hit the floor rug, and he tugged her legs apart, wide. Then he left her there. From the slight stirring of air behind her, she knew he had just shifted.

Julia suddenly realized why he had bought this sofa as the prickle of his whiskers brushed against her thigh. His wet nose pushed into her ass, and he nuzzled in with his hot raspy tongue to find what he was seeking. Julia gripped the sides of the seat cushion, moaning into the fabric as he unrelentingly lapped and laved at her clit. Her entire body broke out in goose bumps of pure hedonistic pleasure. His purring grew louder as he pushed her to the brink. She shoved her hips back, and he lapped harder. Heat rushed through her as the molten pleasure pushed her body to a rapturous peak. His tongue speared deeply into her convulsing channel, lapping at her flowing juices, making her stomach muscles clench harder, pushing her higher.

She screamed into the sofa cushion as her body shuddered in paroxysms of spasms. She lay in a contented bliss for only a few seconds before the air stirred behind her again. He had shifted back, and she felt the heat of Mohan's skin at the back of her thighs and arse. The head of his cock connected with her still twitching pussy. Then he thrust deeply into her. She threw back her head, groaning at the rapturous feel of him filling her, completing her. He gripped her hips and set a frantic pace, pumping in and out of her, over and over again. He knew all the right angles and where to hit all the right spots within her. She loved his talent of being able to propel her over the edge into multiple mind-shattering climaxes.

Mohan let out a loud tiger snarl as he came, pumping his seed deeply into her body. Once his breathing calmed, he wrapped his arms around her waist and pulled her up onto the sofa.

"Vhat was that paper you brought to me?" Mohan asked, once he started to breath normally again.

Julia gave a breathy giggle. "The store in Melbourne has sold all four of your tables--at nine thousand dollars each. And they want more."

"Tell them I be busy vith new home project for a vile. I build tables vhen I can." He kissed the back of her neck and withdrew from her body. Curious, Julia shifted in his arms.

"What home project?"

"Need to build new vroom on house."

Julia gave him a blank stare. "Why?"

He gave her a cocky grin. "Remember how I know you pregnant last time?"

"Oh." Julia quickly clued in. The shed door suddenly banged open, making them both jump. Two sets of curious little pale blue eyes glanced in their direction.

"Mumma, what you doing? We heard noises."

Mohan rolled off the sofa and snatched her shirt from the floor. With a lusty smile of promise, he handed it to her.

"Nothing to worry about. I thought you two were sleeping."

"Raja woke me up." Alex nudged his twin.

"No, mum. Alex woke me up." Raja elbowed him back.

She sighed, gazing with fond affection on her very active three-year-olds.

Mohan found her discarded trousers and tossed them in her direction just as he shifted. Her two three-year-old baby boys' faces lit up as their father pounced playfully towards them. The boys squealed in delight. He dropped his huge tiger body down onto the floor, and the twins were quick to undress before they shifted into their own mini versions of Daddy's tiger and bounded up and onto him.

Julia grinned. She glanced down to her stomach, *another set on their way*.

"Well, it sure beats wasting money on pregnancy test kits."

With a tongue as wicked as Mohan's, why would she ever want to use one? She quickly redressed and went to join the fun.

About the Author

I am a full time mother and part time writer. I live in a small country town in Victoria Australia. I have been writing ever since I learned to read, and almost endlessly drifting off into the fantasy world of my imagination.

Thankfully, I have a great group of supporting writer friends; a husband and three; currently small children who help keep me grounded.

When I'm not day dreaming of creating new worlds for my stories or madly typing away on my laptop. I have plenty to keep me busy on the home front.

I welcome feedback from my readers so please contact me at:
angelacastleleros@yahoo.com

Or visit my website: www.angelacastle.net

Also by **ANGELA CASTLE** at
ROGUE PHOENIX PRESS
http://www.roguephoenixpress.com

BLUE FIRE

A war has left his people on the brink of extinction; Drystan Commander of the King's Warriors will turn to any means necessary to save his people.

Jane, an ordinary woman of Earth, falls into the strange land of muscle bound, sword wielding men, unlike any she has ever seen and what's worse they seem to want her!

Could this woman be the savior of their people? Savior or not Drystan knows what he wants, and he wants Jane.

As the passion starts to sizzle, evil forces threaten to tear them apart. Can Drystan hold onto the woman not only he needs but also his people?

"Angela Castle's *Blue Fire* is a fabulous short novel that had me entertained the whole way through." Lila for *Two Lips Reviews*

STEALING FIRE

Sequel to *Blue Fire*

In the land of the Kell, Tuthal and Tamara are content in their new relationship until Tuthal uses Tamara as bait to steal back the soul he sold long ago.

Adalardo, King of Kell, has found his queen in Penny, an abused housewife from Earth. Adalardo must challenge Penny's husband in order to claim her as his queen.

The soul demon, who is angered over the betrayal of Tuthal, seeks revenge, targeting not only Tuthal but all those around him.

When the demon strikes a blow right into the heart of both men, they must join forces in hope of defeating the evil that has taken their women.

"Stealing Fire has everything you could ever want in a fantasy romance! I absolutely LOVED it!" Regina, Reviewer for *Coffee Time Romance and More*

KEEPING KATIE

Finding love in the boyish home renovator and handyman Jordan MaKensy, dominant lawyer Jack Cullen, will do anything to make their dream of a home and family a reality. When shy Katie starts working at his law office Jack, know he's found something very special, for them both.

Aussie girl Katie has come to London to start a new life for herself after a hard and tragic past. What she didn't expect was to find not one man but two. Katie is swept into a world of sensual pleasure that only two men can provide.

Yet Katie is resisting their attempts to win her heart. Jack and Jordan need to help Katie overcome her fear of love, to let them love and Keep their Katie.

www.ingramcontent.com/pod-product-compliance
Lightning Source LLC
Chambersburg PA
CBHW072237190626
46809CB00018B/2674

* 9 7 8 1 9 3 6 4 0 3 8 3 7 *